The Cry of the Fox

Barbara Evans

ISBN: 9781688722460

ACKNOWLEDGMENTS

A big 'thank you' to my family; my husband for being patient with my I.T. learning difficulties and my children for listening to me 'rabbiting' on about ideas, plots and characters.

THE CRY OF THE FOX

She left the hole in the bank, sniffed the air, turning her head this way and that, ears pricked. Night sounds were all around her: scuttling of tiny creatures rustling the leaves, the thin wind whistling through the bare branches that rattled and scraped against each other, the distant hoot of an owl and the bark of the dog fox on the hill. The night was very cold. Frost would soon crisp and whiten the exposed grass and edge the remaining autumn leaves, that were sprinkled across the path, with a sparkling frosting. But these were of no interest to the young vixen. She trod carefully and delicately, nose to the ground now, following the scent of a wood mouse, her first meal of the night. She continued picking her way through the trees, stopping every now and then to snap up a beetle or leave her scent mark behind.

She loped across the wide open space that ran beside the duck pond...there were ducks sleeping on the bank. She might be lucky!

Much later, as the sky began to lighten in the east she sneaked back to her den tired and still hungry. She had been out of luck tonight.

CHAPTER 1

Roxanne stared glumly out of the bedroom window hugging herself into her huge cardigan. She was cold.

"When's Dad going to get the heating working? We'll freeze to death if he doesn't hurry up."

"Your guess is as good as mine," her brother Rob replied looking up from the football magazine he was reading as he sprawled beneath the duvet on the unmade bed. "Do you want the other duvet? You could wrap yourself up in it like me?" She ignored the suggestion, too absorbed in the view from the window.

"I can't see a single other house from here. It's really wild. I think I'm going to like it, exploring that wood. I bet it's full of birds and animals."

Rob huffed and pulled a face. "I hate it already, unless the school's got a good football team that I can join." He groaned. "Why did we have to leave Newton Heath and move to this empty hole of a place!"

Roxanne turned from gazing out at the frozen landscape and went and sat beside her brother with a sigh.

They were twins. At the beginning of October, two weeks previously, they had been fourteen. Both had freckles and the fair skin that burnt red easily in summer, and auburn hair, though Roxanne's hair was rustier in colour and fell in curls to her shoulders. She mostly tied it back in a scrunchy. Both were tall and slim but Rob was the more athletic of the two. Roxanne loved books and nature. Rob loved football and riding. They had learnt to ride at an early age, at their Grandmother's stables in Wales.

"You know why. It can't be helped. Dad couldn't cope any more in that awful job. I'm glad he was made redundant!"

Rob glared at her. "He wasn't exactly thinking about us though was he? Selling up and moving down here. Leaving everyone and everything we've ever known." He rolled away from her burying himself in the folds of his duvet. Roxanne knew he was close to tears so said nothing.

It was different for her. She had left behind very few friends and nobody she'd really miss. She enjoyed her own company, loved painting and writing poetry. The girls at her previous school thought she was a bit weird and tended to poke fun at her, or ignore her completely, but Roxanne didn't care. She had learnt to be happy in her own skin and didn't need others to affirm her. She knew things would be the same at the new school, but it didn't bother her. The countryside outside was beckoning and she was going to bury herself in it enjoying each and every changing season.

Their mother called from downstairs. "Lunchtime you two!" Roxanne rose and stared down at the lumpy shape that was her brother. "Are you coming? Or are you going to sulk here and starve yourself to death?"

"I'm coming," Rob heaved the duvet off onto the floor and followed Roxanne out of the room clattering down the uncarpeted stairs and into the huge kitchen.

A large scrubbed, wooden table filled the middle of the room and a long Welsh dresser lined one wall, opposite an in-built oven, a gas hob, and microwave, there was also an old-fashioned range with an open fire complete with blazing logs.

"Wow! that looks good," said Roxanne, dragging a chair alongside the blaze. "It's freezing upstairs."

"Dad's fixing the boiler right now, so the heating should come on soon. Have you chosen your rooms?" Their mother, a shorter and rounder version of the twins, brought to the table steaming bowls of soup and then a wooden board holding a freshly sliced loaf of crusty bread, another board of cheese was already on the table.

"We haven't really looked around properly yet. Rob's too grumpy!"

"Oh, come on Rob! Don't be difficult.. Your Dad's doing the best he can. You know he couldn't find work in Newton Heath, at least he's got a chance here. Thanks to his friend Archie."

"Who is Archie exactly?" Roxanne asked blowing her soup to cool it down and helping herself to a slice of bread.

"He was at boarding school with your Dad, before your Dad's family fell on hard times, and they've kept in touch fairly regularly ever since. He was Best Man at our wedding.... lovely chap... Oh there you are Justin! I was just going to give you another shout," she said, turning as her husband came through the door at the far end of the kitchen.

He was a tall, angular man with thick dark hair that sprang up from his forehead. His eyes were a deep brown with crinkly lines at the edges which gave him the appearance of someone who was about to laugh at some secret joke. His hands were large and competent and at the moment very grubby. He was wiping them on an old piece of rag.

"Well, Sally, I've got it going, but we're going to need a new boiler soon. It's very old. I'll just wash my hands and come and join you." He disappeared again through the door. Sally turned back to the children.

"That's good news... About your bedrooms...you'll have to decide soon so we can make up the beds. The furniture van's arriving sometime this afternoon and we will need to know where to put your bedroom furniture."

"I'm in the front," said Rob. "That's where I dropped my bag, and there's a bed in there already and my duvet. I'm not fussy."

"OK, how about you Roxanne?"

"I'd like to look round at the rest of the house. There's another floor isn't there? A tower room?"

"Yes but the stairs are very narrow. I doubt we'd get a bed up there, leave alone a wardrobe. You could use it as a study...somewhere to do your poetry and your painting?"

"I'll go and have a look. I'll start at the top and make my way down. Should be fun. Coming Rob?" He got up from the table and slouched after her.

"Don't think so," he mumbled.

Sally was left sitting at the table, a worried frown creasing her forehead as Justin came to join her.

CHAPTER 2

The house was low and wide, with a short round tower built at one corner, almost like a church. Their friend Archie knew the Landlord and had persuaded him to let the family rent it at very low cost, as it had been unoccupied for several years. Originally built by a keen astronomer, it had a narrow twisting staircase leading from the landing to the tiny turret room that had windows all around. Roxanne stood in the middle of the room entranced, slowly twirling round taking in the varying view.

"This is magic!" she exclaimed. "Too small for a bedroom, but perfect to paint in or write. I might even do my homework in here." She looked around. There were book shelves beneath the broad window sills and on one of the shelves a map. Roxanne opened it up. It was a map of the surrounding countryside, showing the house and driveway, the woods, fields, pathways, a grand building of some sort, the river, right on the edge of the map, surrounding the town of Crowhampton. She laughed to herself delighted with her find, then shivered. It was really cold. "No heating! I'll talk to Dad." She walked carefully down the staircase.

There were four large bedrooms. Two at the back of the house, one had a shower room attached, and two at the front, overlooking the drive. Then there was a roomy family bathroom with a shower over the bath but no curtain as yet. Roxanne decided to take the other front room across the landing from Rob. She liked the view over the wood. As she stood gazing out, the furniture lorry pulled up in front of the house. She yelled to Rob excitedly and rushed down the stairs eager to unpack all her treasured possessions.

Her Dad stood outside directing the men, telling them where to put everything.

"Don't get in the way now Roxy," he said when he saw Roxanne hopping from one foot to the other.

"Can I help with the boxes?"

"It's nearly all furniture in this lorry. There's a smaller one coming with the boxes. You can help then."

The men were very quick, and soon tables, chairs, sofas, lamp-stands, sideboards, television, wardrobes and dressing-tables were all installed in their rightful rooms if not in the correct place. Roxanne knew her mum would be the one to decide each piece of furniture's final resting place. Just as the men were climbing back into their lorry, a large van pulled up behind it. The boxes had arrived.

Roxanne rushed forward looking for the ones with her name on. Some were too heavy for her to lift. These were her books, but again it didn't take long for all the boxes marked 'Roxanne' to be piled higgledy-piggledy around her room like the ruined ramparts of a castle.

The furniture was arranged around the walls, but not where she would like them. She studied the room thoughtfully. First of all, the bed...facing the window, so she could look out at the tree tops and the sky. She pushed and dragged it into position; then the wardrobe...beside the window which was huge and wide; the chest of drawers... on the other side of the window; the writing desk would go upstairs into the turret room. The small bookcase she placed behind the door alongside the small dressing-table. There was even room for a comfy armchair, the room was so big.

Roxanne knelt down beside the boxes and began to open them, books first. She arranged them on the shelves in categories, poetry, novels, natural history, text books for school. Soon the shelves were full. She would take the rest up to the turret room.

Then she unpacked her clothes stowing them neatly in the drawers and the wardrobe. Her mother came bustling in with arms full of bedding. She gazed round amazed.

"Roxanne this is lovely! I love the way you have arranged the furniture. You've done it all so quickly too! Do you think you'll be happy here?"

"I love it already," Roxanne replied smiling. Her mother heaved a huge sigh and sat down on the bed still cradling the bedding.

"I don't think Rob's finding it easy."

"Don't worry Mum, he'll come round. Once he's made friends."

"I hope so." She stood up. "Let's get this bed made up, then you're done. I've only got Rob's to do now."

"Are you and Dad in the room with the ensuite?" Her mother nodded.

"Very nice! I thought you might. Better than sharing with me and Rob in the mornings." They chuckled together remembering the tempers that flared each morning in their old house as they all seemed to need the bathroom at the same time.

"I'll do Rob's bed, then I'd better start preparing dinner. Can you give me a hand?" Roxanne followed her Mum into Rob's room. He was sitting on his bed glowering at the boxes and furniture that lay scattered around him.

"Oh Rob! You haven't even started...Roxanne's finished her room..." but Roxanne interrupted her.

"I've come to give you a hand," she said brightly to her brother, taking the bedding off her mother. "You've got the dinner to do. I'll stay and help Rob." Her mother glared at Rob then left the room, her retreating back speaking volumes.

"I don't want to be here!"

"You've made that obvious. But there's no going back Rob. We've got to make the best of it."

"It's OK for you to talk. You never had any friends at the last school to leave behind." He knew he was being unkind but anger rumbled around inside him and he had to let it out at someone. He didn't feel able to explode at his Dad; the person he saw as responsible for creating this miserable situation.

Roxanne sighed. "I know... But that doesn't stop

you from inviting your friends to come and stay. I bet they'd love it here with the woods and... everything." she ended lamely, eyeing her brother cautiously, half expecting another moan. A tiny spark lit his eyes as her words sank in. He looked up.

"Yeah! I bet they would like it here, and we've got that other bedroom. That's a great idea! Thanks Roxy... Help me get sorted?" They spent the next hour arranging Rob's furniture and unpacking his electronic games, sports equipment, a few school books and his clothes. Roxy made up his bed, then stood looking round at their handiwork.

"Thanks, that looks great, and, I'm sorry about what I said."

"That's OK let's go down and see if dinner's ready. I'm starving."

CHAPTER 3

The next few days of the half term week were spent organising the rest of the house. Roxy and Rob weren't needed till the weekend when they would have to visit the nearest town of Crowhampton to buy their school uniform of grey and blue.

The frost that had descended on the village of Foxham disappeared, and, as is often the case in late October, milder weather swept in bringing with it a light misty rain. Soggy leaves were glued to the driveway and pools gathered in the gutters reflecting the heavy grey October skies.

Roxy and Rob set out to explore the countryside. They headed straight for the woods as soon as the rain stopped.

"Don't get lost," their mother warned. "You don't know how big the woods are."

"We've got a map," Rob yelled waving it in the air. They crossed the road at the end of their drive. At the edge of the woods they stopped and opened up the map. "Let's see if we can find this path." Rob pointed to a path that wound round in a curve through the woods in the direction of the large building named on the map as Overton Hall. They walked along the road until they could see the path clearly, cutting through the tangled grass.

Decaying toadstools sprouted from some tree trunks, sticking out like cream and yellow painted shelves, some crept over fallen branches like an orange plague rash. They passed a steep bank with a deep hole tunnelled into its side.

"Ooh what's that smell? It's rank!" exclaimed Rob.

"Fox," Roxy replied. "I smelt it before when we were at Granny's. Once smelt, never forgotten."

"You're telling me! It's really strong. Do you think a fox lives there?"

"Possibly. It looks like an old badger's sett, but

9

foxes do use them if they're empty."

They walked on. Fallen trees, blown down in the gales, sometimes blocked their path. They either climbed over them, taking care on the slippery bark, or clambered around them wading through the knee-high bracken and scratchy brambles covered with ancient shrivelled blackberries. Eventually they reached a wire fence and a rickety gate that led into a field sloping down to a large duck pond. In the distance they could see an imposing country manor house, standing at the top of the gentle slope. Stately trees of Beech and Cedar graced the lawns surrounding the house and Horse Chestnut trees marched either side of the long driveway.

As soon as they reached the bank, some ducks that had been swimming on the other side began to turn in their direction.

"Oh no," laughed Roxy. "They think we're going to feed them!"

"Sorry mate, you're out of luck," Rob said to the leading duck as he waddled out of the water. Just then they heard the unmistakeable sound of hooves approaching at quite a gallop. A horse and rider came racing down the slope towards them. The horse a glossy bay with mane and tail flying. They stopped, the horse snorting and stamping.

"Do you know you're trespassing?" The rider called down to them in a very cut-glass accent.

Roxanne, ever the peace-maker replied quietly.

"No, sorry, we've only just moved here and it's our first time exploring the surroundings."

"Oh, where are you living?"

"Rowan House, just the other side of the wood."

"Oh!" he said again "I had no idea Dad was renting it out." He slid from the saddle and approached them. He was about as tall as Rob, but slimmer with a mass of black curly hair cropped short and a pair of strikingly blue eyes, that were now sparkling in a friendly manner. He offered his hand in greeting shaking hands with Rob first. "Sidney

Overton-Croft. Everyone calls me Sid. My Dad owns your place."

It was the twins' turn to say "Oh".

"I'm Roxanne, Roxy, and this is my brother Rob." Roxanne said as they shook hands.

"Pleased to meet you. Twins by the look of it. Are you going to the local school? Whose form are you in?"

"A Mr Turner," said Rob not sure he liked this posh-speaking boy who was the son of their landlord.

"Great! That means you're in my form. We need some new blood to stir things up. What's your favourite subject?"

"Football!" was Rob's immediate reply. Roxy laughed.

"That's even better," Sidney replied grinning, posh voice disappearing. "We've got a team...of sorts but we could do with more players. You any good?"

"Not bad," Rob replied modestly.

"Huh!" Roxanne exclaimed. "He was the player that brought our school from the bottom of the school league to winning the cup last Year. They really didn't want him to leave and come here."

The boy's eyes were dancing. "Brilliant! Just what we need." He clapped Rob on the shoulder. "Better go. Wander where you like. See you Monday!" He leapt back on his horse and rode off the way he had come.

***

In bed that night, Roxy tossed and turned, and when she eventually slept, images of the wood flooded her mind. The rank smell of the fox in her nostrils, so strong, woke her. She sat up, and looked around almost expecting to see a fox in her room. Then got out of bed and moved to the window. A beautiful slim fox, silvered by the moonlight, brush outstretched, was walking down their drive. It stopped, turning its head, looking up at her as if it knew she was there. Roxanne held her breath in delight. She was sure the fox could see her and was looking into her eyes, then it trotted off down the driveway disappearing from view. Roxanne returned to her bed and slept.

CHAPTER 4

Saturday arrived damp and foggy. The cobwebs in the hedges transformed into white lace doilies by the misty air. Their Mum drove carefully through the fog, into Crowhampton to buy their uniform. There was only one shop that sold it.

"I hope they have your sizes," Sally said ushering them inside.

The uniform was quite smart with grey trousers for Rob and grey pleated skirt for Roxy, white shirts and blue sweatshirts. They both had to wear ties and pulled a face at the thought.

"I think you'll look very smart," Sally said, admiring the uniform and feeling the quality of the fabric between her fingers.

They also had to have sports clothes. Again, in blue and grey; shorts, tops, tracksuits, knee-length socks. Everything was put into bags and had to be carried to the car.

"We'll go for a coffee now," sighed Sally. "I could do with something to restore me after paying out for that lot!"

"Mum it was a small fortune!" Roxy exclaimed. "Can we afford it?"

"We've got to. Your Dad'll be well paid once he starts work and we've still got some of his redundancy money, although that's going down fast with having to buy curtains for every room. Luckily our Landlord is paying for the carpet on the stairs and in the living room, and he's promised to redecorate as well. But later."

"The carpets are coming today aren't they?" Rob asked.

"Yes we thought it a good idea as we'll all be out of the way." They pushed the heavy door of the coffee shop and went into the warm interior. It was very 'oldy-worldy' with check cloths and a tiny vase of flowers on each table.

Around the walls, high up, ran a rustic wooden shelf crammed with all kinds of Toby jugs, male and female. Roxy was fascinated, trying to decide which one she liked best. A waitress came to their table dressed in a black dress with a frilly white apron tied around her waist. She took their order with a very straight face.

"She only looks about our age," Rob whispered. "Do you think she goes to our school?"

Roxy shrugged. "Maybe it's a Saturday job. Can we have a wander around when we're finished here?" she asked her Mum.

"Why not? I've got some things to get. We'll meet back here in an hour's time." They finished their coffees and left.

Roxanne and Rob wandered up the hill towards the impressive building that was at the top. It turned out to be the Town Hall with a museum, and library attached. There was a Saturday market in the cobbled square outside the building and they wandered around the stalls for a while, but as they sold mostly fruit and vegetables, cheap clothing and craft items that were very expensive, they decided to go into the museum and library.

The building itself was huge, but when they went inside, each section was fairly small with the Town Hall taking up most of the room.

Rob was grumbling. "This is really boring Roxy. Why do you want to visit a crummy museum?

"I just want to see what it's like. It might tell us a bit about the history of this town."

Rob gave a heavy sigh, and screwed up his face. "What's so interesting about that? Can we see if there are any shops that sell games? I want the next 'Mystic Maze', It should be out now and I've still got some money left over from my birthday."

"Can we just have a quick look?"

"OK if you must."

There was a reception desk in the entrance hall so

Roxy went over and asked the man behind the desk where to find the history of the town.

"That's all the way up the top love. You can use the lift."

"Thanks. Come on," she said to Rob. "We'll be quicker in the lift."

When they reached the top floor they were greeted by a huge window that looked out over the town below and the surrounding countryside.

"What an amazing view!" Roxy said, walking over to look out. Even Rob was impressed.

"That's pretty neat!" he said nodding his head. "Look, you can see the woods. Our house must be the other side."

"And Overton Hall which must be where Sid lives," Roxy said.

"Yeah, Posh!"

Roxy moved away from the window and wandered among the glass display units. An ancient map was exhibited against the wall. Roxy studied it for a while.

"Hey Rob, this was the site of an old castle." He joined her and gazed at the map.

"They would have had a great view if enemies tried to attack," he remarked. "Can we go now?"

"OK but I'd like to come back and have a longer look around."

"But not with me!"

They descended in the lift once more and walked outside and down the hill, losing themselves in the maze of tiny streets that branched off from the main thoroughfare. Eventually the streets opened out into another square and here they found a shopping centre that contained all the fashionable shops and department stores, including a shop that sold every electronic game you could wish for. Rob was in his element!

"I'll have a wander," Roxy said to Rob, "while you're in the shop." She sauntered along, glancing in at the shop windows but not really interested in anything, itching to get back to the museum. There seemed to be plenty of interesting artefacts that she would have liked to see if they had had more time. She wandered back to the game shop just as Rob emerged clutching a bag with the shop's logo blazoned across the front.

"Can't wait to tell Mike. He'll be so jealous!" Mike had been his best friend back in Newton Heath.

"Have you heard from him much?" Roxy enquired as they walked back to the coffee shop to meet their Mum.

"Yeah, he texts me about once a day, mostly moaning about how useless the team is without me." His face had fallen into gloomy lines. Roxy wished she hadn't asked.

CHAPTER 5

Monday dawned bright, cold and frosty. The twins were up early, both feeling apprehensive and nervous. Roxanne quiet and withdrawn the way she always reacted when she was nervous. Rob was the exact opposite. He became loud and talkative, giving a running commentary on the new game he had bought and how good he was at it already, punctuated with questions like ---

"what do you think the Games' teacher will be like? Will they let me join the team straight away? Will I have to have a trial first?" He kept on till his Mum told him to be quiet, his chattering was making Roxy more tense.

Their mother, who had registered in the local schools as a supply teacher, drove them to school, she didn't have any supply work that day, in fact it would probably be a while before schools would contact her. Their father had left earlier to begin his new job as Manager at a nearby Retirement Home called The Cedars. They hoped it would go well for him.

They were dropped at the school gates and walked up the drive together aware of all the curious stares coming their way. At reception they had to wait for someone to take them to their new form-room. They sat on some low chairs waiting, very stiff and upright. A woman came through the door, smiling, and addressed them.

"Roxanne and Robert? I'm Mrs Stone, I'm Head of year four. There's no doubting that you're twins. You are very alike. I'll take you to meet your form tutor Mr Turner. You'll meet in his room for registration every morning and if there are any problems he's your first port of call and if necessary he will refer to me. Mr Turner will give you all the books you need." They had stopped outside a door which had a glass window in the top half and Mrs Stone pushed it open. They followed her in. The hubbub died down and twenty-five pairs of eyes swivelled in their direction.

Mr Turner was tall, and well-built, with very short hair, and brown eyes that were alert and direct. 'No nonsense' eyes Roxanne's Granny would have said. He smiled at the twins and raised his voice to address the class, while Mrs Stone left the room.

"Listen up 4T we have two newcomers to the class. Rob and Roxanne Hetherington. I hope you will make them feel very welcome, they've only been in the village a week." The class gave a short clap of welcome and most faces smiled at them. A boy raised his hand. It was Sid, the boy they had met when they went exploring.

"Rob can join our table," he said grinning. "We've already met and there's space." Rob grinned back.

"Great," said Mr Turner. "Now where shall we put you Roxanne? There's a space on Sophie's table I think." Sophie put up her hand and beckoned Roxanne over.

They were given diaries in which they could copy out their timetables, school and homework, and an exercise book for note taking. There was no time to chat and get to know the other table members, a bell went for them to set off for their first lesson which was English. It was obvious that Rob was getting on famously with the boys though, as there was a general buzz of noise around him and Sid. Sophie just smiled shyly at Roxanne and walked with her down the corridor. The other girls more or less ignored Roxy and talked among themselves. Roxanne was not bothered though. She was used to it.

The English teacher was Mr Rose.

"What have you studied so far in English literature?" he asked. "We're quite a way through 'Macbeth'."

"That's what we were doing in our old school," Rob replied.

"Have you kept all your work?" The twins nodded.

"Good. Hopefully it will be relevant. Find an empty seat." They looked around. This room had desks, two per desk and all in rows facing the front. There were two seats towards the back of the room. Rob sat with one of the boys he had already made friends with, Roxanne sat next to one of the girls who had studiously ignored her on the way to English. She had a 'china doll' appearance, pink and white skin, pale blue eyes and straight, dark hair loose to her waist. She was very pretty. Roxanne smiled as she sat down, but the pale eyes remained blank, the mouth set in a straight line...no welcoming smile. Roxanne turned away and focussed on what Mr Rose was saying.

Roxanne didn't see much of Rob for the rest of the day, but at break times, Sophie kept her company.

"You sat next to Melanie in English,"

"Oh is that her name? She didn't speak."

"No she's like that. She thinks she's above most people because she sometimes gets invited to Overton Hall to go riding with Sid." She went pink when mentioning his name.

"Is he the class celebrity?" Roxanne asked, thinking that Sophie probably had a crush on him.

"All the girls fancy him. He's very good at football and makes people laugh. You know," she wrinkled her nose trying to think how to word it. "He's always fooling about, practical jokes, that sort of thing. That's why he was expelled from his boarding school."

"Boarding school?"

"Yeah, his family is very rich as you can imagine. They own, not only the Hall but all the land around the village as well. Apparently Sid played up so much that in the end they expelled him.

"Wow! He must have been bad."

"His parents were really angry with him. There was quite a fuss, because in the past Sid's Grandfather was squire of the village, Lord of the Manor, and his Dad is Master of the Hunt..."

"What's that about?" Roxanne asked.

"I'm not terribly sure as I'm not very interested, but

I think he's the person that decides when and where the hunt can go."

"Hunting live foxes d'you mean, with dogs?... I think that's barbaric. It should be stopped." Sophie opened her eyes wide in alarm.

"I think they aren't supposed to do that now, it's not allowed but I wouldn't speak against it too loudly if I were you," she said softly putting out a restraining hand, thinking Roxanne would leap up and do something daft. "There are a few girls in the class that are part of the hunting scene as well as some of the boys. You wouldn't be very popular saying that sort of thing."

"Who wants to be popular?" The bell went for the start of the next lesson and with a shake of her head Roxanne walked stiffly into registration. Sophie followed at a distance.

CHAPTER 6

They did their homework in the little circular room at the top of the house. Their Father had put a heater in the room and a round multi-coloured rug. Their Mother had given it a good clean and put up some curtains the colour of marigolds which, now they were drawn against the night, made the room feel as if it was surrounded in sunshine. After homework, Roxanne told Rob about her conversation with Sophie.

"Did Sid say anything to you about it?"

"He told me he'd been expelled, and asked me if I'd like to go to the next hunt with all the others. I told him I didn't own a horse, but learnt how to ride when we stayed with Gran. He said I could borrow one from his stable. That's amazing! Being able to ride again." Rob was really excited.

"Would you do that though?" Roxanne asked. "Go and watch a fox be torn to pieces by dogs!"

"I don't think that happens now. I think they shoot it."

Roxanne huffed at him. "Fat lot you know! I told Sophie I thought it was barbaric and it is, and so is anyone who takes part!" She stormed out of the room and thundered down the stairs. Her Father looked up from reading the paper.

"What's up Roxy? You look a bit steamed up. School not good?"

She threw herself into the armchair. "It's Rob,"

"Oh what's he done now?"

"It's not so much what he's done, but what he plans to do." And she poured out the whole story to her Dad who listened sympathetically.

"Yup," he said. "It is a cruel sport and it used to go on all over the country as a country pastime, but I think you'll find it's been banned. The Act comes into power next February. They follow a trail now, not a live fox."

Roxanne shook her head.

"Well that's good," she said grudgingly, "but Rob said they shoot the fox once it's caught, so they must chase it! And that's horrible too.... I'm going to bed." And with that she left the room just as her mother came into the living room to join her husband by the fire.

"What was that all about?" Sally asked, eyebrows raised.

"Roxy's got herself all steamed up about fox hunting. Rob's made friends with a chap at school who's invited him to the next hunt." Sally pulled a face.

"I'm not surprised she's all steamed up. You know her passion for nature and wildlife. This will really cut across everything she holds dear. Especially if her brother supports it. I think we're in for a rough ride." Rob came in and noticed his parents' gloomy faces.

"What's up? You said you got on alright at work." He looked at his Father.

His Dad shook his head. "It's not that. It's Roxy."

Rob sat down on the sofa next to his Dad.

"yeah, she's wound up about me going with Sid to the next hunt... She says it's barbaric."

"Well Rob, you know what she's like. She loves the countryside and the animals. Hates to see anything hurt." His mother appealed to him.

"Yeah, I know, but Sid's a great guy, his Dad's our landlord by the way." He hurried on seeing his parent's eyes open in surprise. "He said I could ride one of his horses... and do a try out for the school team. All the guys are great and they all go to the hunt. It's a big thing round here, and I want to be a part of it. It's different for Roxy, she prefers animals to people...always has."

"I know what you mean, Rob, your friends have always meant a lot to you." His father leaned towards him. "But do your best not to antagonise Roxy. This is a really sensitive issue for her to deal with."

"I won't mention it if she doesn't, but you know

what she's like, once she's got the bit between her teeth, there's no stopping her. She'll be on at me day and night!"

"We'll talk to her, if that starts to happen. Off to bed now it's late."

Rob slouched out of the room, his excitement evaporating and a slow anger rising up within him. Why did Roxanne have to go and spoil things? He was just thinking he might like it here after all. He could see that Sid and the others would be good mates and they certainly wouldn't have anything to do with him if he took the judgemental attitude that fox hunting was wrong.

It's alright for her he thought angrily she's a 'loner', enjoys her own company, she can take the 'high ground'. Then as suddenly as it came, his anger went and he felt miserable. He flopped down on his bed and stared at the ceiling. They had always got on so well in the past, yes they quarrelled now and again, but underneath that, there had always been a deep bond of acceptance and understanding. That bond was under threat now. They were on different sides of the 'fence' and there was no way either of them would budge. It was as if an invisible and impenetrable barrier had come down between them and Rob could see no way through.

He undressed and put on his pyjamas still trying to work out how they could come together again but no ideas came except the fact that the hunt would be following a trail not a real fox! Maybe Sid could convince her that basically the hunt was just a mad gallop across country. Feeling slightly less anxious, Rob rolled over and fell asleep.

Because of her row with Rob, Roxanne slept fitfully with thoughts of what he was getting involved in flooding her mind. She was not convinced about trail hunting and suspected that they preferred to chase a live fox. Rob had always been quite soft-hearted in the past and seemed to love animals as much as she had. Moving here had changed him. Surely Rob could see that it was cruel to chase an animal, creating such terror and desperation then finally death. Her heart ached for the animal and raged at the people who couldn't understand, or wouldn't understand how inhuman their actions were. She slipped into a dream...

She was racing across country and up a slope, terror gripping her as the howling voices drew ever closer, knowing she would die if they caught her.

The shrieking bark of a fox woke her from her dream with a start. Sweat was causing her hair to stick to her neck, but she wasn't too hot, it was the sweat of fear. She took deep breaths to slow her racing heart, then getting up she tip-toed to the window expecting to see the fox strolling down their driveway again, but it wasn't there. They'd better not chase my fox she thought as she climbed back in bed, before falling asleep once more.

CHAPTER 7

Breakfast next morning was a very silent affair. Roxy wouldn't even look at her brother. Resentment smouldered in her eyes. Rob ignored her. In the car on the way to school their Mum gave them a talking to.

"Now, look here both of you, we've just been given this chance to start a new life. I understand it was hard for you Rob to leave your friends behind and you're keen to make new friends here, and that's good, I'm pleased for you.

"Now Roxy I also realise that animals and birds mean a lot to you, but just because you have different views and opinions as it were, I'm not having it disrupt the peace in our home. You've got to make up your minds to be civil to each other. I would prefer the subject of hunting not to be mentioned if possible and certainly no continual arguments about it. Neither of you know the whole story yet and I would wait before you both make up your minds as to where you stand on the issue. Now do you understand?

"Your Dad's coming to terms with a new job and we need to support him by making home a happy place for him. He doesn't want to come home every night to bickering children!" Roxy turned her head to Rob in the back seat and gave him a stony look.

Rob could see the stubborn look on her face, but answered mildly "OK Mum, we get it. Sorry Roxy. We won't argue anymore."

"No, sorry Mum. We won't." Roxy added.

Roxy made up her mind to avoid the subject as much as possible, especially in school because it made her so angry she knew she wouldn't care what she said or did. It boiled up inside her turning her stomach into knots. As a result, the rest of week at her new school passed quite peacefully.

***

25

On Friday night, the fifth of November, a firework party was taking place in the village on the cricket field. Sophie had told Roxanne about it and asked if she would like to go, the whole village usually turned out. When Roxanne shared this news with the rest of her family it was decided that they would all go.

The night was very dark with only a crescent moon amidst wispy clouds, but luckily there was no rain. There was a large crowd of people and it didn't take Rob long to disappear with the lads from school. Roxy soon found Sophie and stood with her at the barrier that had been erected to stop people wandering into the firework area. There was music in the background, a bar in the pavilion and various hot-dog, and hamburger stands. The atmosphere was very festive.

The fireworks began promptly at seven thirty with a whoosh of rockets that exploded with white and gold stars and loud crackles like thunder. The crowd all 'ooohed!' and 'aaahed!' This was followed by a display of fireworks resembling flowers in a garden, and so the evening continued with a fine display of Roman Candles, huge Catherine wheels, rockets and gentler ones like Golden Rain for the tiny children that were present.

Roxy watched the faces around her illuminated by the different coloured light from the fireworks, now a rosy red, now a brilliant white, a chilling blue and warm orangey gold. She decided she'd like to do a painting capturing the expressions and the colours.

The display over, Sophie returned to her parents and Roxy pushed through the dense crowd searching for hers, when all at once a loud crackling erupted amongst the feet of the people in front of her, who began to scream and leap out of the way of something that was fizzing, sparkling, and jumping about on the ground. A Jumping Jack! Roxy was standing near a fire bucket of sand which she grabbed, and threw the contents over the dancing firework which immediately went out. Some people cheered, others laughed. She turned and came face to face with some of the lads from her form and Sid who looked furious, his mouth in a thin angry line.

"What did you do that for? It was only a bit of fun."

"Huh!" Roxanne scoffed. "By the sound of it, not many people were laughing. I did hear some screams and a few tears from the little kids. It was a stupid thing to do!"

"What gives you the right to dictate what goes on at our village firework party, you've just got here...from the town."

"What gives you the right to frighten people just because you're the Lord of the Manor's son. How feudal!" Roxy was trembling with rage. She turned on her heel and strode off through the crowd.

Sid stood for a moment equally angry. No girl had ever spoken to him like that before. They usually fell at his feet. Then his anger cooled and an amused smile hovered momentarily across his face. He re-joined his friends and laughed the whole incident off.

Roxy caught up with her parents who had been looking for her, and Rob, who obviously had not been involved in Sid's stupid game. They found their car and drove home. Roxy didn't tell them what had happened, but knew Rob would find out soon enough.

That night, Roxy spent the last hour before bed researching on her mother's computer, as much as she could, about the subject of fox hunting and the ban that would be put in place in February. Some people suggested that it didn't go far enough and would make no difference at all and hunting live foxes with dogs would still go on in some areas.

***

On Saturday Rob was collected by Sid's Mum to take the boys to football. She was a short woman, with very smart clothes, and wavy, shiny blond hair, the exact opposite of Sid. She was not at all 'posh' or stand-offish and chatted to Sally in a friendly way. Rob went off full of suppressed excitement.

Roxanne had asked if she could go into the town to do some shopping, wanting to look round the museum and library. There was a bus every hour. Her Mum was pleased that Roxy was confident enough to attempt visiting the new town on her own.

"I've got my mobile if I need you," she assured her Mum. "But I'm sure I'll be OK."

"It'll be the same bus you'll have to catch on Monday as I've been asked to teach at the primary school in the next village, so it'll be good to get to know the route it'll take. Have you got enough money?"

"Yes thanks." Roxanne wandered off down the drive to wait at the bus stop.

The ride to town was quite interesting to Roxanne as it meandered through the country lanes stopping first outside the school gates then on to the village, stopping by the pub and at the end of lonely farm driveways. The trees were mostly bare of leaves except a few stubborn oaks and beeches that seemed to cling onto their leaves as if afraid to show their naked trunks and branches. Puddles lined the road blinking, now bright, now dark, in the fitful sunshine, reflecting the sky. Sheep still grazed in some fields awaiting the birth of their lambs in February, and a squadron of rooks flew overhead... speeding away on some unknown mission. This was the countryside that stirred a deep satisfaction in Roxanne. It excited her and moved her in a way that nothing else could. She wanted to pick it all up and embrace it, keep it safe and beautiful for ever, and with that thought came a deep sadness. She knew it was not possible and that the countryside had a dark side too...death as well as birth.

Soon the bus was travelling through neat suburban streets of detached then semi-detached houses, followed quickly by Victorian terraces, corner shops, busy streets and the small bus station.

Roxy alighted shouldering her back pack and paused to get her bearings. She wasn't at all sure how to reach the narrow twisting street that led up to the Town Hall, museum and library. Looking around she could just see the Town Hall, sticking up above the roofs, in the distance, crowning the hill. So she made her way in that direction, passing quickly through the square that was crowded with people going in and out of the big Shopping Centre. She reached the tiny streets that would join up with the one that led to the Town Hal.

These streets were full of interesting small specialist shops. She passed a shop that only sold coffee and tea, one that only sold cheeses, a flower shop, a wedding shop, and several interesting Charity shops. She worked her way through these tiny streets up towards the Town Hall. Outside were the usual market stalls. Roxanne wandered through, stopping every now and then to look at the things that were being sold and then came upon a stall that had anti-hunting posters draped over the front and pinned to display boards at the back of the stall. Roxanne hesitated. Would it be a mistake to stop? She wondered. Then made up her mind and went closer.

CHAPTER 8

A young man with longish brown hair that flopped over his forehead sat behind the table reading a newspaper and smoking a cigarette, flicking the ash absent-mindedly into his empty coffee cup. He quickly folded up the newspaper and looked up when he became aware of Roxanne standing there.

"Hi, what can I do for you?" he asked, smiling.

"I'm not really sure," a hesitant smile played around her lips.

"Coffee?" he asked, waving a flask in the air. He produced a mug from under the stall and proceeded to pour her a cup. She gazed at the posters. Some, really cute pictures of foxes and their cubs. Others, with savage slogans across them, of dead foxes that had been killed by the hunt, the bodies held up as trophies. Then there were pictures of the local hunt itself, again with angry slogans slashed across the images.

The young man passed her a steaming mug of coffee which she accepted gratefully.

"OK then, my name's Harry and yours?"

"Roxanne Hetherington. We've just moved here from Newton Heath."

"We?" he leant forward inquiringly.

"Mum, Dad and my brother Rob. We're renting a house in Foxham." She sighed, finding it more difficult to explain than she expected.

"Well, as you can see," he waved his arm vaguely towards the posters. "We are devoted to stopping the awful blood-sport of fox hunting, and have had some success. We still need to make sure people who break the law are brought to justice. Is that what you're interested in?"

"Of course!" she exclaimed vehemently. "I had no idea when we moved here that that sort of thing went on!" Words began to pour out telling him how she really felt about the natural world and how important it was to protect it and keep it safe, and to her dismay she could feel the prickling of tears behind her eyes. She stopped, taking a deep breath. He was listening very intently, his face soft, his brown eyes gentle with understanding. He groped for another cigarette and lit it. The smoke curled up from between his lips.

"How old are you?" He asked gently.

"Fourteen," she replied.

"Well, at the moment fox hunting can still go on, it doesn't really become law until eighteenth of February next year, but there's nothing to stop you turning up out of interest, plenty of kids do."

"I'm not a kid," Roxanne objected stiffly.

"I didn't mean to offend you; it's just being an adult starts at eighteen."

A young woman arrived at that moment. She was short with closely cropped fair hair that gave her an impish look. Huge hoop earrings swung from her ears. She wore a long, loose-fitting coat.

"Hi, who's this?"

"This is Roxanne, she's only just moved into the area and hates the thought of fox hunting."

"Welcome to the club," the girl said, extending her hand which Roxanne grasped in a friendly hand-shake. "I'm Marie by the way. Has Harry filled you in on what we've been doing?" Roxanne nodded.

"I think I would like to help in whatever way I can."

Harry got up from behind the table. "I'll leave you two to it then, I've got to go and talk to the printers about the leaflets for the next hunt." He grabbed his scarf that draped the back of his chair and wound it around his neck.

"Nice meeting you Roxanne. See you again no doubt." And he disappeared into the crowded Saturday market.

Marie pulled out the chair and sat down making a face when she saw the contents of Harry's coffee cup.

"Cigarette ends in coffee dregs! Disgusting habit! Wish he'd give it up, he knows it could kill him." She looked directly at Roxanne her head on one side. "Come and sit down while I fill you in." she said patting the chair beside her. "The ban comes into force next year. But in the meanwhile fox hunting can carry on as normal. We try to disrupt the hunt as best we can, and sometimes it gets a bit rough. The hunt people become really riled and use their riding crops occasionally."

"Actually hit people you mean?"

"Yes and charge at us with their horses. So I really think it would be better if you didn't involve yourself in that sort of thing, but you could help in distributing leaflets and generally spreading the word that we need to keep protesting in spite of the ban."

"I'm not afraid." Roxanne assured her. "How do you disrupt the hunt anyway?"

"We take along things that will make a noise. We even have our own hunting horn, and the noise confuses the dogs and we hope they'll lose the scent. If you do turn up, you'll have to stay well back especially if it gets a bit rough. Do your parents know about this?"

"Not yet, but I still want to be involved somehow, even in a small way."

Marie chuckled. "Good for you. But you do need to talk to them. Where abouts do you live?

"Foxham."

"Wow! Enemy territory!"

"What d'you mean?"

"Lord Overton-Croft leads one of the biggest hunts around here. Since the ban, he's been following a trail to be fair, but sometimes a fox might cross the trail, and when that happens, the hounds go after the fox. It's called an 'accident'. So we tend to turn up in case there's an 'accident' and try to divert the hounds. He's wealthy... and powerful! Anyway what do you think?"

"I'd like to join in and do what I can, but I'll have to

talk to Mum and Dad. I don't think they'll be too happy about it though."

"We usually have a stall in the market and distribute leaflets to passers-by, take donations and try to get people to sign another petition. You could help us pass out the leaflets if you like, even if you don't get to come to the hunt itself. Have you got a phone I could text you on?"

Roxanne scribbled her number on the piece of paper Marie handed her then caught sight of the time from the Town Hall clock. She rose quickly to her feet.

"I'd better get going. I said I was going to the museum and the bus home leaves in half an hour. I would like to think things through before I tell my parents everything. They don't always see things the way I do."

Marie chuckled again. "Do they ever? Well I hope we see you again. You know where to find us." She handed Roxanne a card. "That's our phone number if you need to contact us."

"Thank you." Roxanne stuffed the card into her pocket. "Bye". She turned and made her way towards the Town Hall. Marie stared after her a thoughtful expression on her face.

CHAPTER 9

Roxanne did not want to tell her parents or Rob where she had spent the morning, so knew she would have to look around the museum so she could chatter about it a bit. Rob would be full of the football try-out so hopefully he would dominate the lunch time conversation and would not notice her silence.

When she reached the museum she went straight to the top room and studied the artefacts in the glass cases. Stone-age flints, bronze arrow heads, the blades and hilts of ancient weapons. This hill had obviously been a place of fighting from the very earliest of days...or maybe a place of refuge, a fortress where people ran when threatened by an enemy and these weapons were used in their defence. Whichever way it was this had been a place of violence.

Once past the glass cases, she came to a model of the town and the surrounding countryside. It was a bit battered and worn in places and had obviously been made several years previously. It represented the town and countryside during the time of Elizabeth the First. There was no Town Hall crowning the hill, but the ruins of an ancient castle instead, the town itself much smaller, the houses thatched and some were the usual black and white Tudor dwellings. The river flowed around the outskirts of the town and there was a mill beside it near the bridge. An imposing Abbey lay at the foot of the hill, where the church now stood, as you would expect. The woods were more extensive and the Manor house was clearly shown only it was much smaller with tall twisted Elizabethan chimneys. The house that Roxanne lived in with her family was not there. It must have been a much later addition.

Roxanne wandered on keeping an eye on the time. She didn't want to miss her bus and she had quite a walk to the bus station from the top of the hill. The next section was all about Legends, Curses and Witches. She was going to pass it by when the word

'Fox' caught her eye.

There was the strange tale of a woman called Old Mother Reynalds whom the villagers suspected, had the ability to change into a fox at night and went about raiding her neighbour's chickens. A hunt was organised to catch the fox, but when they caught up with the hounds, expecting to find the body of the fox, they found the dead body of Old Mother Reynolds. Had she changed into a fox or had the hounds been following the wrong scent? No-one ever discovered the truth. There were other similar stories but none with so detailed a written record. These stories disturbed Roxanne as she remembered her vivid dream, that had felt more real than ordinary dreams. She left the museum with the stories rooted in her thoughts.

Her mind was in a whirl all the way home on the bus. It was raining heavily now and the windows were blurring the landscape and turning it into an impressionist painting, but Roxanne had only eyes for the images and pictures inside her head, turning over all the things that had been said about present day fox hunting all mixed up with the legend of Old Mother Reynalds and the fox.

Roxanne jumped off the bus as it pulled up outside her driveway and raced for the house, the rain soaking her jacket and hair. A delicious smell of hot soup greeted her as she made her way down the hall and into the kitchen.

"Raining is it?" Rob asked her grinning. Roxanne pulled a face at him. Her mother handed her a towel from the clean laundry basket.

"Here, rub your hair, you're dripping everywhere." A bowl of rich vegetable soup was placed in front of her.

"How did it go?" Roxanne asked her brother, knowing the conversation would be settled now for the whole of the meal, and it was. They were told in detail about the trials. Mr Turner was there of course, as Games Master, and it seemed he soon greatly appreciated Rob's undoubted skill. He was given the place of a mid-fielder for the time being, till he got used to the other team players. Rob was hoping he would eventually be a forward so he would have the opportunity of scoring goals. Sid was thrilled and thought they had a good chance in the tournament with him in their team, and the other boys had invited Rob to join in a friendly game of football the following afternoon.

"As long as you've done all your homework," his Father said.

"How about you Roxanne, did you have a good morning? Apart from the rain." Roxanne told them about her finds in the museum, but she didn't tell them about the fox hunting stall or the legends. She still felt disturbed by them although she wasn't sure why.

For the first time since they had moved, Rob felt he was going to be happy. He had a place and was making good friends. The guys on the team welcomed him with open arms. He sent a text to his old friend Mike who text him back moaning that his old team were still doing really badly, but saying he was looking forward to coming to stay the weekend when it could be arranged.

Sid had told Rob about his argument with Roxy at the firework party, but because Sid seemed to think it was a bit of a joke, Rob didn't mention it to Roxy. Things felt more friendly between them at the moment and he didn't want to spoil it.

They spent the afternoon finishing off their homework in the tower room. Then Roxanne sketched out her idea of the faces at the firework party. Everything seemingly back to normal.

CHAPTER 10

Sunday afternoon, with Rob off to play football with some of the boys from school, Roxanne put on her coat and boots, wound a scarf around her neck and set off for the wood. The map was stuffed into her pocket so she would be able to find her way back. She wanted to climb Brock Hill. It looked like a monk's tonsure on the map with the trees growing around the slopes leaving the top bare.

Roxanne passed the fox's den once more and was assailed by the strong smell bringing with it memories of the legend and her dreams. The path branched, and checking with the map, she took the left hand path. Soon it began to rise quite steeply, winding in and out among birch and ash trees, with the occasional hawthorn red with berries.

Great craggy stones heaved their shoulders through the scanty turf when, on reaching the top, she emerged from the trees. Roxanne looked all around, then sat down on a flat boulder to take in the view. The massive expanse of sky spread out all around her with grey, purple and white clouds tumbling around. A Red Kite soared above, its wings stretched out on the surface of the wind, a black crow cawing raucously was trying to chase it out of the sky. The Red Kite sailed on imperturbable, unflappable. Roxanne took out her note book and jotted down words and phrases she could later weave into a poem. The Red Kite was inspiring; the way its wings were spread taut surfing the air currents. The crow like a ragged beggar harrying a king.

Because she was so high, she could see part of her house, the turret stuck up above the trees like a round, church tower. The bare branches hid the ground floor and driveway. The house seemed cradled by the trees like a cosy nest thought Roxanne. Gazing in the other direction she could see Crowhampton and the church spire.

All around were fields, some containing sheep, nibbling the grass in contentment; some had been ploughed up and were already sprouting the next crop in dark green stripes; and others were ridged and brown like corded velvet having been ploughed and the next crop not showing yet. Some black stocky cattle were grazing in one field, a bright green patch among the duns and blond of bleached grass. Roxanne scribbled her thoughts and feelings into her notebook.

Around her feet, the grass was closely cropped by rabbits, their black marble droppings in plentiful evidence. She folded her arms across her chest, hugging her coat to her, the wind, knife edged against her face.

Stuffing her notebook into her pocket, she began to navigate her way down the slope, picking her way through the shrubs. A robin was singing its sibilant song on a nearby bush. She stopped and looked but couldn't see him. The sweet sound emphasised the stillness of the woods.

As she arrived at the edge of the trees she could hear the on-coming roar of a car and at the same time saw the fox step into the road. She shouted, but too late, the car hit the fox and sent its body flying onto the opposite verge. There was a shriek of brakes then the car reversed slowly. Roxanne was kneeling over the body of the fox, stroking its fur.

"What the devil were you doing jumping into the road like that, I thought we'd hit you?" Roxanne looked up tears of rage in her eyes. Sid was standing there with an older man, who had obviously been the driver.

"I didn't jump into the road. I yelled at the fox to warn it. You were driving much too fast!" She was gathering the fox into her arms. She could see it was a vixen. "She's not dead."

"She soon will be," Sid remarked callously. "Her back's broken, she can't move her legs."

"We could get help. "Roxanne suggested.

He laughed derisively. "Don't be ridiculous! It's a

fox...vermin. Nobody bothers about them like that in the country. You wouldn't understand coming from a town. The shame is it'll be one less to hunt!"

"How can you be like that! It's a beautiful wild creature!"

"Yes, and it's dead!" Sid replied leaning in close and looking into the fox's eyes as it gave its final shuddering breath. "So you might as well leave it where it is."

"I'm not," she replied. "I'm going to bury her."

Sid shook his head. "You're crazy. Come on Uncle Gary, let's go." He turned towards the car.

Gary hesitated. "Can we give you a lift home?"

"You can't be serious!" Sid exclaimed in irritation. "Carrying that stinking fox in the car.".

Roxanne looked up unable to hide the tears that were pouring down her cheeks. "I'll be OK, I'll ring my Dad, he'll come and fetch me." She fumbled in her pocket for her mobile.

"If you're sure," Gary said frowning, then turning away to follow Sid.

Tears were wetting her cheeks feeling like icicles, in the freezing wind as she spoke to her Dad, explaining where she was and what had happened. Roxanne waited patiently, holding the dead vixen close.

CHAPTER 11

After a while her Dad's car drew up beside her. He jumped out.

"Oh!" he sighed looking at Roxanne cradling the dead fox, tears trickling silently down her face. "Is he dead?" he asked gently, leaning in to stroke the rusty head. Roxanne nodded dumbly. "What do you want me to do with him?"

"It's a she Dad...a vixen. Can we bury her? In the wood somewhere...somewhere she would be familiar with?"

"That wouldn't have to be the wood. I bet she roamed all over the place. We could bury her beside our driveway amongst the trees. I expect she visited there often enough." Then Roxanne remembered the fox she'd seen trotting down their driveway. She nodded her head.

"Yes, please,"

"OK, get in. Do you want me to put her in the boot?"

"No... I'll hold her on my lap."

"She does smell a bit Roxy,"

"I don't want her in the boot like some piece of rubbish."

They climbed into the car, her Dad turned it in the road. They set off home in silence.

Justin went immediately to the shed and brought back a spade. Roxy's Mum came out to see what was going on. She stopped when she saw Roxanne standing by the trees holding the fox in her arms its thick bushy tail hanging down past her knees. She approached Roxanne cautiously knowing how upset she would be.

"How awful!" Sally exclaimed. "Such a beautiful creature. How did it happen?" Roxanne gave a weary sigh.

"Hit by a car. It was Sid. He was horrible!"

"He wasn't driving surely?"

"No, but he was in the car, and he was horrible!"

she repeated.

Justin arrived carrying the spade.

"Come on then Sweetheart. You choose the place." Roxanne led the way pushing through the undergrowth until they came to a small clearing.

"Will you be able to dig there under that beech tree? There may be bluebells in the Spring."

"I can try." Justin went to work. He was a strong man, having worked out doors for much of the time. In spite of the roots that spread out beneath the tree, he was able to dig a good sized hole.

Roxanne placed the body of the vixen reverently in the hole, and knelt in silence beside the little grave for a few moments looking down at the brightness of the rusty coloured fur and slender black legs, her thick brush curled around her body as if keeping her warm.

Roxanne's Mum went forward and rested her hand on Roxanne's shoulder. Justin scooped up a spadeful of earth and quietly spread it over the vixen's body. Roxanne watched as spadeful after spadeful began to hide the vixen from view. When she was completely covered and there was just a small mound to mark the spot, Roxanne turned away with her Mother and walked back to the house, her Mum's arm around her shoulders.

CHAPTER 12

It was dark by the time Rob returned. He was full of the great time he'd had with the lads and how he'd been able to show them a few excellent moves. After chattering on for some time it suddenly dawned on Rob that Roxanne was very quiet and just staring down at the kitchen table. "Did you have a good afternoon?" he asked puzzled. Roxanne shook her head and rose from the table.

"I think I'll get on with the rest of my homework." She left the table and they heard her hurrying up the stairs.

"What did I do?" Rob frowned looking at his parents.

"It's not you," his Dad smiled ruefully at Rob. "Roxanne found a fox that had just been hit by a car. It was still alive, but died. She carried it back insisting we bury it in the trees at the edge of the drive. She's very upset."

"Ooh! That's really bad, considering how she feels about foxes in particular."

"The thing that made it worse as far as Roxy is concerned, is that Sid was in the car and made some very unhelpful comments." Rob's face was a picture of gloom, his mouth set in grim lines.

"I'd better not mention the hunt then."

"Rob, we agreed!" was Sally's anguished cry of alarm.

"I know Mum, but I had to let you and Dad know somehow. There's a hunt planned for next Saturday and I want to go. I have to have your permission."

Sally and Justin looked at each other, neither very happy about it.

"I'm not sure that I agree with fox hunting with dogs," Justin said.

"They're not chasing a fox Dad, someone goes out early laying a trail and the hounds follow the trail."

"Mmm! Well I suppose that's OK. What time do

you have to meet up?"

"I've got to be at Sid's by nine fifteen, to collect the horses, then ride down to the pub in Foxham to meet up with everyone else. Oh and it'll cost fifteen pounds."

"Knew there'd be a catch," Mum smiled. "As long as you're careful and don't fall and get trampled by one of the huge horses..." she glanced at her husband, he shrugged.

"We don't see why you can't go. See what it's like. I suppose you'll have to wear your smart riding jacket."

Rob grinned "Sid's going to lend me a cravat thing. Thanks Dad, I won't mention it to Roxy if I can help it. Although she shouldn't mind as we're not chasing a fox. I'd better finish my homework too." He left the table and made his way upstairs.

Roxy's door was open; she was standing gazing out of the window into the darkness.

"Sorry about the fox," he muttered.

She turned at the sound of his voice and heaved a huge sigh.

"I don't remember being so aware of death when we lived in the city."

"We never saw it except on TV," Rob replied. "Those nature programmes you couldn't bear watching."

She smiled a sad smile then and sat down in the big easy chair. "They were horrible, watching animals catching and eating other animals."

"That's nature, Roxy, foxes catch and eat all sorts of other animals... and birds."

"Yes, I know. It still makes me angry though when human beings do it when they don't have to...killing for fun and driving too fast on narrow roads. She didn't stand a chance! Sid was in the car Rob, and he said some horrible things about them being vermin." Rob stared at the carpet feeling uncomfortable.

"He doesn't realise how you feel Roxy."

"It's not about me Rob. It's about a beautiful wild

creature's life being snuffed out...and not caring or thinking it's worth anything." She turned away. There was a long silence.

"Well, I'm going to finish off my homework." Rob said eventually. "Have you done yours?"

"Just going up." Roxy heaved herself reluctantly out of her chair and made her way up to the turret room. Rob followed.

***

In bed, that night Sid turned and tossed. He could not get to sleep, visions of the paths and woodland trees haunted his thoughts. He believed that he could even smell the dankness of the rotting leaves and feel the drip of moisture on his coat. He jumped awake at that thought, imagining he had a coat of fur!

Getting out of bed, he went to the window, full of a strange longing to leave his room and wander freely through the woods. "This is crazy!" he muttered to himself, but when he closed his eyes the images returned as vividly as before. He was close to the ground, nosing his way through the brittle bracken and brambles which just combed his thick coat lightly, his brush low to the ground, his ears pricked picking up every rustle and whisper of sound. Sid was aware that he was desperately hungry too and needed to catch something soon to satisfy his hunger.

He opened his eyes instantly, shaking the images from his head and returned to bed. After a while he slept, his dreams troubled by the bark of foxes on distant hills and woodland walks under the stars searching for prey.

***

He padded softly down the drive in and out of the trees, keeping to the shadows. The house behind him looming in the darkness, no light to be seen. A crescent moon shone briefly between heavy clouds that scudded across the sky. At the road he hesitated, turning his head this way and that. He sniffed the air. An owl hooted distantly and the scent of rabbit came strongly to his nostrils. Loping across the empty road, he headed through the trees and up the slope where Roxanne had walked the other day. He could smell Roxanne's powerful human scent and for a moment confusion filled his mind and made him question why he was there at all, and then the smell of rabbit came to him and he pushed on forcefully up the hill.

Reaching the top, he crouched, belly to the ground watching and waiting. Several rabbits were cropping the short grass contentedly. He watched for a while before striking. It was too easy, one of them had come so close there wasn't even a chase. He nipped its neck and it hung loose and dead in his jaws. Turning he trotted back to his den to feast in peace.

Satisfied, he proceeded to lick any blood off his coat. There were some pieces of rabbit left for the following morning. It had been a big rabbit, more that he could manage in one night. A Dog fox barked shrilly causing his ears to rotate towards the sound, but he was not interested in fighting just yet, he knew the young vixen that had lived in this part of the wood was dead. Having finished his meal, he curled up into a ball and tucking his bushy tail around him he settled down to sleep.

Sid woke feeling really cold. He was lying curled into a ball on the top of his duvet. As he was waking, he wriggled around expecting his bushy tail to pull closer, then jumped up startled at the action which felt natural and automatic. What am I doing here? He thought, images of his underground den starkly vivid before his eyes. Then he remembered the rabbit and shuddered, sure he could still taste its blood in his mouth. He stared in horror, his fingers and bare feet were muddy, a dead leaf clung between two of his toes, he shook it off, trembling, then made his way to the bathroom to rinse the taste from his mouth, and wash his hands and feet. That done, his mind in terrified shock, returned to his bed and tried to warm up, thinking over every detail of his night time prowl, almost too frightened to sleep.

CHAPTER 13

On Monday, Rob and Roxanne had to catch the bus to school as their Mother had a day's supply teaching. They sat in silence, Roxanne gazing out of the window at the dreary, dripping landscape. The sky was low and steely grey, a soft misty rain soaking everything. They swished through the roadside puddles occasionally sending up a fine muddy spray.

Every time Roxanne closed her eyes she could imagine the vixen pushing through the wet undergrowth, hurrying to the safety of her den and settling down in the dry and warm earthiness to sleep. Opening her eyes, she'd take a deep breath and try to block the images from her thoughts, but they were always there in the background.

"Are you OK?" Rob asked. "You keep shutting your eyes as if you want to go to sleep. Did you have a bad night, thinking about...you know...the fox?"

"A bit, but nothing unusual," she lied.

They pulled up outside the school, and were soon engulfed in the crowds of young people all thronging through the gates. Rob joined his friends. Roxanne pushed through on her own. She could not bring herself to join in the aimless chat that surrounded her, and she definitely didn't want to talk about the fox. She struggled to concentrate during her lessons, longing to be outside, not cooped up in a classroom, in spite of the drizzly weather.

At lunchtime she sat at a table to eat her sandwiches and Sophie and a few other girls joined her. Roxanne was determined to make more of an effort to be friendly, especially to Sophie, realising that she was being rude ignoring everyone. She listened attentively and smiled in all the right places, she hoped, but again had difficulty in following what they were talking about most of the time. Then she was aware that Sid and a crowd of girls and boys were drifting past their table on the way out, but had stopped when Sid saw Roxy. He looked straight at her.

"Did you bury it then?" he said with a smirk. She glared at him.

"What if I did? It's no business of yours!"

"What happened?" Melanie asked. But Roxanne was too preoccupied with looking daggers at Sidney to reply.

Sid answered. "Just a fox, my uncle knocked down accidentally, but it died. Roxy found it and decided to bury it."

There was a general snigger of amusement.

"Bury a fox!"

"Why not? You were driving too fast. You must have seen it crossing the road and you didn't slow down!" Roxy's voice was cold with suppressed anger, her fists clenched.

Melanie shrugged and sent Roxy a puzzled look.

"But they're vermin aren't they? Didn't your uncle do us all a favour?" she smiled up at Sid.

"No he did not," Roxanne spoke through tight lips emphasising each word. Her whole body tense as if to spring at Sid.

"Yeah but when the fox hunting ban comes in, they'll become a real nuisance, so my Dad says," Tom, one of the boys, chipped in.

Roxy exploded addressing them all in loud, angry tones. "What is the matter with you people! Can't you appreciate the uniqueness and beauty of a wild creature and accept the way it lives without wanting it dead!" Another of the boys spoke up.

"You wouldn't understand, coming from the town. You haven't seen the mess a fox makes when he gets in among the chickens. Heads and legs torn off and thrown about the place." Some of the girls squealed at this description. "It's obvious he kills for fun!"

"There's quite a lot of that around here! And I don't mean foxes." Roxanne retorted rising from the table and stalking off. She didn't want anyone to see the tears of rage brimming in her eyes.

"Did I say something?" Sid asked playing the innocent. The girls tittered appreciatively gazing at him with adoring eyes.

Later, when Sid met up with Rob, he told him all about the encounter

"Your sister gets quite 'wound-up' when it comes to foxes doesn't she, considering she's always lived in a town?" Sid muttered to Rob.

"She's always been the same about wild life, potty about nature and particularly wild animals and birds."

"Potty's the word for it. Does she know about Saturday?"

"No, not about me joining in. My life won't be worth living," Rob sighed. "I'll be for the High Jump."

"She does realise that we're following a pre-set trail doesn't she? Unless a live fox crosses the trail, of course?" Sid grinned wickedly, opening innocent eyes.

"The subject is taboo in our house."

"Well it's been ages since we chased a fox. It would be great if a live fox crosses the trail on Saturday 'cos the dogs will be after it then and no stopping them."

"Have you ever seen how the dogs kill the fox?"

"Ages ago, I was about six. The dogs went mad, the Master tried to get them back but couldn't. It was a real mess by the time I got there, turned my stomach to tell you the truth, but I was only six. Mum dragged me away. I think they tried to shoot it before the dogs got there but they were too late... I suppose your sister has a point. But it's all so much a part of country tradition, I can't imagine them stopping it altogether."

Images of that awful day flooded Sid's mind for a moment. The fox's body torn and spilt, the hounds tearing, the excitement of the hunters, their gleaming eyes glistening with exhilaration as if they had achieved something wonderful. He felt the nausea rise to his throat.

"You OK mate you went a bit white then?" Rob's concerned face brought him back from the brink.

"Yeah fine."

The bell went for afternoon lessons. They all trooped off for registration.

CHAPTER 14

On Tuesday Roxy received a text from Marie informing her of the hunt to be held by Lord Overton Croft on Saturday. The hunt was meeting outside the pub in Foxham. The saboteurs were going to be there just in case a fox crossed their trail. They invited Roxy to join them but only if her parents knew and agreed. She would have to stay at the back of the group and not get involved if trouble broke out.

Roxy didn't know what to do. She knew her Mum and Dad would not agree if it involved violence in any way at all, but she wanted to go with all her heart, firmly convinced a live fox would be chased and wanting to do anything she could to stop that happening.

She made her way downstairs as soon as she had finished her homework and taking a deep breath went into the living room where her Mum and Dad were watching the television.

"Can I talk to you for a moment?" she asked hesitatingly.

They both looked up at her anxious face. Her Dad pressed the button on the remote and the TV went off.

"Of course," he said budging up on the sofa to make room for her. Roxy sat between them staring for a moment at the rug.

"Come on, spit it out," her Dad encouraged her.

"Well, when I went into town on my own," she began. "I met these people who are against fox hunting and do all sorts of things to try to stop the fox being caught." Her mother's face was a picture of horror, but her Dad asked calmly.

"What sort of things?"

"They turn up at the hunt and if a fox is being chased they make a lot of noise to distract the hounds so they lose the scent. Anyway, there's a hunt on Saturday and they sent me a text to see if I wanted to go along with

51

them." Sally and Justin exchanged worried glances. Roxanne hurried on.

"I'll be quite safe. They won't let me be in the front. I've got to stay at the back with the people that just go to watch the hunt and make sure that they follow the trail. I'll be quite safe," she repeated... "What?" she asked seeing the uncomfortable expressions on their faces. Her Dad patted her knee.

"It's like this Roxanne, Rob is going on that hunt with Sid and his family." He held up his hand to stem any outraged comments that were forming on her lips. "He asked us at the weekend and we said yes. Sid's lending him a horse and you know how much he loves riding, and he's good at it. They are not hunting a live fox. They're following a trail, so we couldn't see the harm in it."

"I don't believe it! How could he! My own brother!"

"Roxanne, it'll just be an exciting gallop across country. No fox will get hurt."

"OK, so I can go too then as an observer!"

"That's different!" her mother butted in. "The group you want to be involved with are going with trouble in mind, and I don't want you getting involved. I can't imagine they will be very welcome and are obviously hostile to Lord Overton Croft. And what's more, he's our Landlord!"

"So, I get it, Rob can go, on the side of the high and mighty Lord Overton Croft, but I can't, as I'm on the side of the victim, who happens to be a defenceless animal! Great! At least I know where my family stands in all this. So much for a new life in the country...death you mean!" She stalked from the room amidst distressed cries from her mother.

"Let her go," Justin said to Sally. "I'll try and have another chat with her when she calms down."

"What are we to do though?" Sally asked.

"I'll think of something," Justin assured her.

CHAPTER 15

Roxy was furious and paced up and down her room. She didn't go to find Rob as she knew she was far too angry and any argument might deteriorate into a fight, so would achieve nothing except even more hostility and unrest in the family. It's like we're at war, she thought...civil war... and we're on opposite sides. Live and let live her Gran would say and normally Roxy would be the first to agree, usually the peacemaker, but not in this she thought, not in this!

She grabbed her phone and sent off an angry text to Marie saying she wasn't allowed to go, then curled up on her bed, closing her eyes and trying to subdue her furious thoughts.

***

All the next day Roxy felt her anger growling away inside and images of the lovely fox she had held as it lay dying, kept coming into her mind. She was inattentive in her lessons and had no energy to make any attempt at joining in the general chatter of the girls in her class as she had slept badly. She wandered off on her own at lunchtime and sat gazing out across the school field, an intense longing to be out of the school and its confines and to be wandering through the woods and fields. She was just drifting off into another day-dream when Sophie called her name.

"Are you alright Roxy? You look very washed out." She sat on the bench beside her, her face creased with concern. "They'll let you go home if you're not well."

"I'm just tired," Roxy turned to her and gave a tight little smile. "I'm not sleeping very well. I think it's because it's so different here, in the country, not at all what I expected, I'm not used to it."

"I think it would be the same for me if I moved to

the town." Sophie assured her. "Is," she hesitated. "Is Saturday bothering you? I know you hate the idea."

"Umm...a bit. Rob's going, he's a good rider. Sid invited him. I'm not allowed to go. I wanted to join the protesters."

"Oh Roxy that's so dangerous! They get very violent sometimes. I'm not surprised you can't go."

"Are you going?" Roxy asked her.

"Only to see them off. My Dad's quite keen on 'the British way of Life' as he puts it." She hesitated again. "What does your Dad do?" she asked, to change the subject.

"He's Manager at a Retirement home called the Cedars. An old friend of his owns it, and offered him the job, when he heard that Dad had been made redundant."

"That's amazing! My Nan is at The Cedars. She became very nervous after a fall and was afraid to be by herself. She loves it there and says if she'd known it was so good she'd have gone to live there earlier. Maybe you could come and meet my Nan she's ever so nice and knows lots of stories about the countryside, you know, old folk tales and stuff like that. Dad tells her she ought to write them all down." Roxanne's interest was stirred.

"I think I'd like that," she said. "My Gran is amazing too, she owns a stable and even though she's quite old, she manages it really well and helps out sometimes too. She loves horses, and whenever we go to stay we go riding. That's how Rob and I learnt to ride. We've been riding since we were five."

"Wow! You should really try to make friends with Sid. He's got lots of horses." At the mention of Sid, a cloud seemed to pass over Roxanne's face. Sophie bit her lip.

"Sorry, I shouldn't have said anything."

"That's alright," smiled Roxanne, setting aside her dislike of Sid, and feeling more cheerful. Maybe Sophie's Nan and her stories would lighten her mood even more.

"When do you visit?"

"It's usually a Sunday afternoon, sometimes we take her out for the day, but that's usually on a Saturday. Do you really want to come? She'd be so pleased to see a new face."

"Yes, I really would, I'll ask Dad."

"Oh we'll pick you up. I know where you live. Do you want to come this Sunday?"

"If that's alright,"

"I'm sure it'll be fine. I'll text you." The bell went for afternoon lessons so they returned to the class room.

CHAPTER 16

"I need to talk to you," Roxy said to her brother when they reached home after school. "Let's go up to the turret room." Rob followed her up with heavy steps, dragging his school bag behind him.

"OK, what do you want? I'm not staying home from the hunt, if that's what this is all about." Roxy flopped down into one of the easy chairs.

"It's not really, it's just I can't cope with not knowing what's going on. I know you want to go with Sid now, but I want you to be able to tell me. I hate secrecy and I'll tell you if I'm allowed to go with the protesters, so there's no surprises."

"Are you joining the saboteurs? Roxy that's mad!"

"Mum and Dad won't let me at the moment," she replied bitterly. "But I will keep on trying."

"They can get really rough apparently. And not only that, you'll be setting yourself against our Landlord! He won't like that."

"I don't really care. I just want to do something to make people see how awful it is killing foxes like that."

"Look," Rob said. "I'll talk to Dad and see if he'll let you come on Saturday and you'll see for yourself that they aren't chasing a live fox. They are just following a trail and have been for the whole of the season so far. Sid said they didn't chase a live fox last year either!" He appealed to her. "Roxy, you don't have to be so screwed up about this, you're worried about something that's not going to happen."

Their mother's voice drifted up the stairs.

"Tea's ready! Are you not hungry you two?"

"We are!" they both shouted together. They smiled tentatively at each other, both glad of the truce.

After tea, Rob was as good as his word and went to talk to his Dad. He explained everything to him assuring him that there was hardly any chance that a live fox would be involved on Saturday.

"I think Roxy should come on Saturday, to put her mind at rest, she's getting in such a state, for no reason at all."

"Well I don't want her mixing with the protesters."

"She doesn't have to Dad, not if you came too, you could keep an eye on her."

"Mmm, I suppose I could, if you think it's a good idea."

"Dad, I think it would be brilliant! She'd really see for herself that it's just a great cross country gallop. She might even be persuaded to join in next time."

"Huh, I doubt that very much, but we could give it a go. I'll talk to her."

Roxy was amazed that her Dad had changed his mind.

"Did Rob talk to you?" she asked.

"Yes, he did. He thought it would be good for you to see for yourself that no live foxes are chased."

"I'm not sure Dad. You won't let me join the protesters will you?"

"No, you'll have to stay with me. We're just going to see them off and maybe go again later to see them return. Prove to you that they don't chase live foxes. Does that sound OK to you?"

Roxy puffed out her lips "I guess it'll have to do. Thank you, it's definitely better than nothing." And then she remembered Sophie's Nan. "Oh Sophie will be there. She's a girl from school. She said I could visit her Nan with her. Her Nan lives at The Cedars Dad."

"Oh, do you know her Nan's name?"

"Lawson, I think, the same as Sophie's"

"Oh I know Mrs Lawson, a lovely old lady, very chatty most of the time and happy. Why do you want to visit her?" He looked in surprise at Roxy.

"Well," Roxy didn't really know what to say. "She knows a lot a folk tales and legends ... and I'd quite like to hear what she has to say. And she likes talking to people, so Sophie says, so I thought it would be nice to go and see her...with Sophie."

He shrugged "I don't see why not. If you think you'd like to. I'm glad you've made a friend. Invite her round here some time."

"I might, thanks Dad."

CHAPTER 17

It was still dark when Rob, full of excitement clattered downstairs eager to be ready to meet up with Sid and the others. His mother came into the kitchen in her dressing gown to see what was going on.

"Rob it's only seven thirty. What time are you due at Sid's?"

"Nine fifteen. I'm going to help him saddle up and that."

"You've got ages yet." She turned, giving him a backward glance. "Don't burn the place down," she said as she saw him setting the frying pan on the cooker. "I'm going back to bed. It's Saturday!" He grinned at her retreating back and set to work putting bacon and sausages in the pan. He was soon joined by Roxy.

"I could smell the bacon from my room. Is there enough for me?"

"Yup, get a plate." He shovelled crisp bacon and sausage, that was burnt on one side, onto her plate, while he fried some eggs. Roxy watched him as he concentrated on the eggs, flipping them over, his tongue sticking out between his lips. He was always so full of energy giving himself completely to the moment. There was no mystery with Rob he was always open, what you saw, you got. She wished she could be more like him, but she found sharing her thoughts and ideas difficult because they always seemed to be different from what others thought. Her English teacher at their other school said it was the 'poet' in her.

"Here you are," Rob waved the frying pan in her direction and a slippery egg slid expertly onto her plate. He sat down opposite and picked up his knife and fork. "How do you feel about today?"

"I'm not sure. I'd rather it wasn't happening at all. It'll be funny being there and just watching them set off. I still won't know if they keep to the trail."

"But I'll be there. I'll tell you...promise."

"And I don't know what Harry and Marie will think if they see me."

"They'll understand Roxy. They said themselves you couldn't get involved, and they'll see Dad and know he's there to keep an eye on you. Anyway, I'm sure the whole thing will be just a mad gallop like Sid said. Can't wait to ride, Sid's lending me a horse called Nightmare, she's a great horse apparently. Do you want to come over with Dad and me and see the other horses and ponies? Then we can all go down together save Dad coming back for you."

"Mmm, could do. I don't want to see Sid though. See what Dad says." She finished her breakfast and went to wash up her plate.

***

Sid was awake early too. Through the window he could see the sky lightening in the east. The garden emerging from the darkness in shades of green, the long grass under the hedge bleached and bent over, stems broken by the heavy rain or trodden down by animals. A picture of a red fox slinking by under the shrubs came into his mind as he gazed out. Again, his senses came alive, as they were assailed by the scents of the wet grass, the feel of the dampness beneath his paws, his bushy tail caressing the tall foliage beneath the hedge. His eyes closed as he took a deep breath breathing it all in. What's going on? he thought, and remembered that awful day when he was small. The brightness of the blood on the grass, his father trying to smudge some on his face, his terrified screams.

***

Roxanne was day-dreaming again, wondering what the day would bring and hoping against hope that any fox in the area would stay out of the way.

"You alright?" Her brother stood beside her, his plate in his hand.

Roxy's eyes flew open. "I'm fine. It's going to be a clear day with some sunshine for a change." She smiled at her brother. He nodded in agreement.

"Good day for a ...ride!" he said washing his plate and racing out of the kitchen. "I'll go and get ready."

When Justin arrived for breakfast Roxy told him what Rob had suggested, about going over to Sid's and seeing them saddle up. He thought it was a good idea as long as Roxy was OK with it.

"I'm not too keen, but it'll save you a trek back here."

So that's what they did.

***

Roxy refused to get out of the car when they arrived at Sid's, just watched the goings-on through the open window. Sid was quite surprised to see her. He smiled mockingly.

"Changed your mind?"

"No, and never will," she replied, looking away from him.

Her attitude intrigued him. His usual charm didn't seem to work on Roxy.

"It's OK," said Rob. "She's not come to ride, even though she's a much better rider than me. Just to watch us all set off."

"You'd be very welcome to join us," Sid said sarcastically. Roxy shook her head not bothering to even look at him.

There were a lot of people milling around the courtyard giving her curious glances, and several ponies and horses stamping and champing at the bit. Some held by grooms waiting for their riders to appear. Just then a tall burly man emerged from the front of the house accompanied by Sid's mother. He walked straight over to Justin his hand outstretched in welcome.

"Justin!" he exclaimed. "Good to see you. How are

you settling in? Joining us for the hunt?"

"No, no," Justin shook his head. "Just brought Rob and Roxy." Justin signalled for Roxy to get out of the car and be polite. She did reluctantly and they all shook hands. Sid grabbed Rob by the shoulder.

"Come and meet Nightmare," he said.

"Yes, run along you three have a look at the horses." Sid's Dad commanded. So Roxy, with dragging steps had to follow Sid and Rob round the side of the house to the stables. Several horses were staring over their stalls into the yard. Some tossing their heads in excitement. A groom was just leading a tall black horse out from one of the stalls.

"Meet Nightmare!" Sid was obviously very proud of this beautiful animal. Several other horses were stamping restlessly in their stalls.

"They always know when something's going on and they don't like it if they're not involved." Sid approaching the first stall where a tall bay was snuffling and blowing and tossing her head. He spoke softly to her stroking her long nose.

"Not today Rosie," he muttered. "I'm riding Hero."

Roxy was stroking the pony in the next stall, a gentle looking grey with huge eyes and a blond mane.

"Rob said you were a better rider than him. You could come and ride here with us if you like."

"I don't think so... Thank you anyway." Her reply was decidedly frosty.

Sid shook his head in exasperation and turned to Rob.

"Do you want help saddling up?"

"I think I'll remember how to do it," Rob said with a grin. Roxy moved from stall to stall petting each horse in turn. They were all very fine animals.

"How many horses do you have?"

"About twenty in all. My mother runs the riding school. That's why we have such a range from tiny ponies to big hunters. What did you used to ride?"

"A chestnut coloured mare called Conker..." Roxy grinned suddenly, her face transformed by the joyful memory, and for the first time Sid saw an impish sense of humour peeping out from behind her eyes.

"I get it!" he laughed. "Horse Chestnut...Conker"

The sound of baying and barking reached their ears, breaking in on their shared joke, causing Sid to instantly freeze, his face rigid like a mask. Terror and panic flooded his very being. All his senses on full alert, his mind racing, which way to run. The scent of the hounds strong in his nostrils, the sound like a hammer in his head. Then a voice calling his name and someone shaking his arm.

"Sid, what's up? It's only the hounds. You're not afraid of dogs are you?" Rob was grinning. "You looked really scared for a moment."

Sid blew out a deep breath and gave a shaky laugh as a groom handed him the reins of a beautiful chocolate brown horse with a white blaze and coat like gleaming silk.

"I'd better not be, there are about forty of them," he said leaping easily into the saddle.

The forecourt of the house was a 'sea' of brown and white as the hounds milled around eager to be off. Rob mounted Nightmare and followed Sid, looking very smart, even though he was only wearing his tweed hacking jacket and old jodhpurs. Some of the grown-ups were in the usual bright red coats, the colour, for some reason, called Hunting Pink.

Roxy looked up at Rob. "You look great," she said, smiling up at him. "I thought some of the boys from our class would be here."

"We're meeting them outside the pub... Oh, looks like we're off. See you later!"

Everyone began to trot off down the drive, in the direction of the village of Foxham. The brown and white sea turning into a fast flowing river of wagging tails.

CHAPTER 18

Roxy and her Dad followed behind, as the Hunt moved off, driving very slowly. Her Dad looked sideways at her.

"You OK Pet? Where did you disappear to?"

"We went round to see the horses and ponies. Sid's mother runs a riding school. They've got lots of lovely horses. Sid said I could go and ride whenever I liked. I wouldn't have to pay."

"Would you like to do that?"

"I would love to ride but not Sid's horses."

They soon reached the village and to Roxy's amazement there was a huge crowd gathered to see the Hunt off. There were families with small children as well as teenagers and older folk. She glanced around to see if she could see Marie or Harry but couldn't spot them in the crowd. Then she saw Sophie and called out to her.

"Oh Roxy, you made it." She came over, smiling.

"This is Sophie, Dad, you know, I told you, her Nan lives at The Cedars."

"That's right," Justin said. "You're Mrs Lawson's granddaughter."

Sophie smiled. "Can Roxy come with me next time we visit? My Nan loves meeting new people. Especially young people she says they're always so cheerful." Justin laughed.

"I'm sure Roxy'll do her best." A round woman with curly brown hair and bright blue eyes like Sophie's approached them.

"There you are," she said addressing Sophie "I wondered where you'd got to." Sophie introduced her Mum and they all shook hands.

"So, you're Roxanne. Sophie told me you'd like to meet her Nan. I'm sure she'd be delighted. She loves relating the old tales from around here and Sophie tells me you're interested in that sort of thing. Well, would you like to come with us tomorrow afternoon?" Roxanne nodded and looked at her Dad.

He smiled "That's fine by me."

Justin and Mrs Lawson began to chat, soon joined by Mr Lawson, a tall thin man with a military moustache and bearing. Sophie and Roxanne took in the scene before them. Roxanne recognised several of the girls and boys from her form. Tom was there and Graham and James. Melanie made straight for Sid as soon as she saw him, sidling up on a tall, black pony, looking very smart. Roxanne noticed Fliss and Poppy paying Rob quite a bit of attention, she grinned to herself. The Landlord and the barmaid brought out trays of drinks for the riders and a toast was made.

At a word of command from the Master of the Hunt, who was Sid's father; the hounds moved off followed by those on horseback. Soon the road before the pub was silent, empty of the sound of horses and hounds, just the murmur of the crowd and then the revving of engines as people began to disperse. Roxy and her Dad said their goodbyes, Sophie promising to pick Roxanne up the following afternoon. The bright sunshine striped the road blinking in and out of the tall trees that edged their way home.

***

Darkness had wrapped itself around the house. The curtains were drawn and they were sitting down at the large kitchen table, encapsulated by the pool of light from the overhead lamp, having their tea when they heard a car door slam and Rob rushed in through the front door shouting his 'thank you' over his shoulder and bringing with him a great gust of the wild, cold, night. Roxy shivered, glad to be indoors and cosy.

Rob's cheeks were red with cold and excitement, his eyes shone with delight.

"Oh Roxy, you must come next time. It was great! A tremendous gallop. Loads of hedges and fences to jump.

You should have seen Nightmare go!" He demonstrated with his arms. "Up and over, steady as a rock when he landed. You'd really love it. Wow tea! I'm starving." Everyone laughed at his enthusiasm, as he dished up for himself a large helping of casserole and three dumplings.

"We didn't see a fox, by the way," he shot a glance in Roxanne's direction. "I don't know who laid the trail, but we went for miles. The hounds got really excited at one point and the guy in charge of the hounds and the whippers-in had a job keeping them together for a while, but it was soon sorted out and we were off again. You must come next time Roxy, you really must."

"I don't think I could join the Hunt even though they're only following a trail, but Sid said I could come riding with you whenever I wanted to." Rob raised his eyebrows.

"Are you friends now then?"

"No... not really."

"Right, you two," their Dad butted in. "Time to finish your homework if you've had enough tea." They both groaned and pulled faces as they reluctantly left the table and made their way upstairs to the turret room.

"Have you got much to do?" Rob asked.

"I've got to finish that essay on Macbeth about witches and curses."

They reached the room, the curtains were still open showing a black sky sprinkled with millions of tiny points of light. Roxanne stood and gazed up, her mind turning to what it must be like for a fox, out there in the night, out there among the distant trees with nothing but green things all around, and fresh cold air ruffling her fur, and cold damp earth beneath her paws. She sighed and forced herself away from the window, grabbing the curtains and pulling them closed across the view. Rob was talking, she hadn't heard a word he had said.

"Sorry Rob, wasn't listening."

"I just said I'd used the notes at the back of the play

and looked up a few things on Mum's computer downstairs."

"Did it say anything about these days? You know curses that work, even today?"

Rob laughed derisively. "Don't be daft. That's all superstition. People really believed in the supernatural in the old days, ghosts and things, probably fairies as well." He hesitated then, seeing her serious face. "You don't believe any of that stuff do you?"

"No, of course not. It's just there was a legend I read about at the museum about an old woman who was able to turn into a fox. I suppose it's just living here, deep in the countryside with wild things all around us, even though we can't see them most of the time, it just feels a bit...spooky sometimes."

"It's your imagination getting the better of you. Although, talking of spooky things, Sid was a bit odd when the hounds arrived. He suddenly looked really terrified...just for a moment, and then he was OK again. Perhaps wild things are getting to him too." He shrugged turning to the maths exercise he had to finish.

CHAPTER 19

"I'm going for a walk," Sid announced after breakfast. "It's far too nice to be cooped up indoors."

His mother looked up in surprise. "Walk? That's unusual for you isn't it?" Sid shrugged.

"Just feel like it."

"Be back in time for lunch." He made his way down to the duck pond and hurried towards the wood. As soon as he entered the trees he felt the change take place. The shrubs shot up on either side of him as he shrank, falling forward onto his arms as they transformed into the slim agile legs of a fox. Sid's heart leapt with joy as he padded through the undergrowth taking in the sweet strong scents that surrounded him. The musky dampness of the loamy soil beneath his pads. He felt excited, his body lithe and supple, his legs strong. He sniffed the air, drinking in every scent with anticipation and delight.

Loping along through the trees and out into the fields beyond, keeping to the hedges, then back past the duck pond. The ducks were all out in the middle enjoying the winter sunshine. They quacked raucously when they saw him. But he wasn't interested in them this morning. Sid pushed his way through the hedge into the horse field. They lifted their heads as he passed but otherwise took no notice. Ahead was a farm, and in the farm there were chickens. He was not particularly hungry as he remembered he had dined on rabbit the night before, but he was curious about the netting, how high it was; could he jump? Could he tunnel underneath? Sid was aware that he had visited before but been unsuccessful in entering the run where the birds were kept.

The farm dogs were in the yard and caught his scent setting up a loud barking and growling. He turned tail and fled as he heard the farmer come out from the farmhouse cursing and swearing at the disturbance. He was carrying a long gun and pointing it at Sid. There was a loud bang and the ground in front of him sprayed up, stones, grass and soil spattering his coat as he ran. Another bang, but behind him this time. He was out of range. His heart beat in terror as he tore up the hill, weaving in and out of the trees. He had forgotten about guns! Reaching a dense thicket, he flopped down panting, to catch his breath. The sun filtered through the bare branches striping his coat. He spent some time grooming himself before moving off back to his den, a deep hole among the roots of an aged oak tree on the outskirts of the wood. He'd go out tonight and see what he could find...rabbit, pheasant...chicken, if he was careful.

***

Roxanne was out walking too, and from the top of the hill in the wood she saw the fox running for his life and jumped when she heard the loud reports from the gun. The horses, in the nearby field, were startled too and tossed their heads, cantering around the field in agitation. She walked down the other side of the hill and found herself in a small plantation of fir and spruce. She could see the small scrapes in the soil where squirrels had been searching for their buried nuts. The ground beneath the trees was scattered with fir cones, some chewed by mice or rats. The rank smell of fox was strong here too, maybe the one she had seen running for its life. She found a narrow track through the bronze bracken that led in the direction of home and soon found herself above the den where the vixen had lived and not far from the top of the hill again.

***

When Sid finished grooming he could feel the pull of his human life once more and he was aware of the changes taking place. Leaving his den, he reared up on his hind legs, his arms lengthening, fur and tail disappearing. He shook with the strangeness of it all and had to sit still for a while trying to gather his wits. What was happening to him? Was he going mad? When the dizziness stopped he rose to his feet and made his way home on shaky legs.

Roxy, from her vantage point, saw him crossing the field by the duck pond in the direction of Overton Hall. There was something odd about him that at first she couldn't put her finger on. Then realised he was walking with head and shoulders bowed, not the usual confident stride that she associated with Sid. He looked unhappy.

The sun had moved towards the west. Roxanne realised she would be late for lunch and was supposed to be going with Sophie to meet her Nan. She raced towards her home, bursting through the door into the kitchen where the rest of the family were gathered round the table.

"We were just going to send out a search party," her Mum said. "Enjoy your walk?"

"Yes, I walked a long way, forgot the time...sorry." She went to wash her hands. On returning, Roxanne made short work of the wonderful roast that her mother put before her.

"Where did you go exactly?" Sally asked.

"Oh, across the fields, up to the top of the hill. I saw Sid. He didn't see me. He'd been out walking too."

"Sid walking! Not on a horse! I'm surprised," exclaimed Rob who didn't enjoy walking as much as Roxanne.

"I'd better go and change. Sophie will be here soon."

Fifteen minutes later, a horn tooted outside the house. Sally went out to meet them and introduced herself then shouted for Roxanne who came rushing down the stairs. She went to put on the coat she had worn that morning but her mother took it from her shaking her head.

"Wear the other one. I'll give this a wash it smells of fox."

Roxy put on her other jacket, wound a scarf around her neck and ran out to the car, waved at her Mum and then they were off.

The Retirement Home was a half hour drive away

on the outskirts of Crowhampton. Sophie and Roxy chatted about their homework for the whole of the short journey.

The building was impressive with a wide frontage full of windows looking out onto the driveway and the flower borders which contained colourful shrubs like red and yellow stemmed Cornus and winter flowering viburnum. The front of the house was bright with the golden flowers of winter jasmine. They drove round the side of the house to the car park, parked, and walked back to the front again.

The entrance hall was like the foyer of a large hotel with a reception desk and rooms leading off, a wide imposing staircase and lift to the next two floors. A low table bearing a beautiful flower arrangement was to their right. The carpet was deep pile and the atmosphere warm and friendly.

The receptionist greeted Sophie and her mother by name, with a cheerful smile.

They made their way up the stairs rather than use the lift, and along the corridor to the right. Sophie's Mum knocked on a door and pushed it open.

"Hello Helen, how are you?" Sophie's Nan had a cloud of white hair that framed her heart-shaped face. Her eyes were a deep blue, not faded at all like some older people. Her mouth was curved in a wide welcoming smile. She switched off her television and stood to give Sophie a hug.

"I'm fine," she said, giving Sophie's Mum a peck on the cheek.

"And who's this you've brought to see me?"

"This is my friend from school, Roxy, she's only just started at my school and is very interested in foxes and your stories and folk tales."

"Umm, are you now?" She gave Roxy a shrewd look. "Hair the colour of a fox's coat." Roxy's eyes widened, as she went forward to shake the old lady by the

71

hand.

"I'll put the kettle on and we can have a nice warm drink. I've bought some scones as well. We can have them later." She switched on an electric kettle that stood on the work top in the tiny kitchenette and reached down another cup and saucer from the cupboard above, to join the three that were already on a tray.

"Is it warm enough for a stroll around the garden afterwards? I like to get out as much as I can and it's far nicer walking with friends than on your own. Not that there's much to see but the new man is keen to make the beds and borders interesting all year round."

"That's my Dad," said Roxy.

"Really, such a nice man. Knows his stuff about plants. I've given him a few tips myself though. I used to be a great gardener." Sophie's Mum helped bring the tray over to the coffee table, and Helen told Roxy all about the garden she used to have before her fall. Then the conversation turned to Sophie and school. Roxanne let it all wash over her as she tried to work out how she was going to bring the conversation around to the legend she'd read in the museum.

CHAPTER 20

A watery sun was attempting to shine when they finished their tea. Sophie's Mum helped Helen into her coat and they all trooped downstairs again to have a short tour of the gardens before the light faded.

"I'll show you the flower bed I do a bit of work on," Helen said to Roxy. "Your father was amazed at what I'd managed to do. It's quite big bed." They followed the paved pathway around to the back of the big house where there were a number of raised beds with attractive stone walls. Several could be reached from a standing position and some, a bit lower that could be reached from a wheelchair. Small trees had been planted at intervals and there were benches at strategic points where there was a view overlooking an ornamental pond and fountain, although the fountain wasn't playing at the time.

"This is where I like to spend my time when the weather is nice." Helen gestured to a large circular bed with a paved area all around it and two benches against the walls of neighbouring raised beds. It looked very neat and well-kept, small silver leaved ivy plants were trailing over the parapet at intervals, and clumps of green shoots were already piercing the black soil, the brown and brittle stalks of fuchsias remained from a Summer long gone, but the deep green leaves of the hellebores promised an abundance of snow-white blooms judging by the fat buds. There was a small shrub in the middle with masses of pink flowers.

"What's that lovely smell?" Roxy asked.

"That's my Daphne. It flowers in the Winter and has that wonderful perfume. Your Father was surprised when he saw it. It's quite tricky to grow. I'm rather proud of it." She smiled a cheeky smile. "The bed's not much to look at, at the moment," she said leaning forward and pulling out a tiny weed. "But it'll soon be a picture in the Spring."

"It really is lovely when things start to come up." Sophie's Mum said. "We'll just walk down to the pond Helen, and then we'd better go back as it's getting colder and the light is fading." Sophie tucked her arm through her Nan's as they walked down to the pond.

"And then can you tell us one of your stories? I'm sure Roxy would love to hear one." Helen smiled at Roxy.

"One about a fox maybe?" she raised her eyebrows as she looked at Roxy. Roxy smiled back.

"That would be great, thank you."

When they got back, Sophie's Mum made another pot of tea to have with the scones that were set out with cream and jam. They settled themselves comfortably, rubbing their hands in the warmth of the gas fire.

"Well now, where shall I start?" Helen gazed at Roxy, her head tilted to one side.

"Well..." Roxy hesitated. "There's a story in the museum about a woman who they thought could change into a fox."

"Oh, that one. Rowena Reynalds." So Helen began the story of Old Mother Reynalds, putting in a lot of extra detail that had not been included in the museum.

"Old Rowena was a widow and lived on the outskirts of the village of Foxham. She was considered to be wise in the healing properties of plants, and people would come from all around for potions and balms that would give relief to their various ailments. She could even heal the ailments of sheep and cattle. They always paid her in whatever they had in the way of food; sometimes a bag of flour or a loaf of bread, a pat of butter or some vegetables from their garden. So, she lived on the goodwill of her neighbours and was very well respected until a new family moved into the village and the father claimed to have the latest in modern medicine for everyone as well as their animals.

He called himself a Doctor and set up a consulting room and people began to visit him instead of going to

Rowena and they claimed his cures were much more successful. As time went on and Rowena grew older, she found it hard to keep herself fed. Her small garden was too difficult for her to dig and she no longer had visits from grateful neighbours asking for her potions and ointments.

Then one day, she found a wounded fox in the woods, it's leg appeared to be broken and there were wounds along his side, and being a kind and loving woman she took the fox in and nursed it back to health, using her ointments and medicine. When the fox was well it went back to the woods but visited Rowena frequently, sometimes bringing her a pheasant or a rabbit, almost as if it knew how badly off she was in the way of food.

In those days people were very suspicious of old women who lived alone and as time went on they forgot about all the good things Rowena had done for them and when it was discovered that a fox was visiting her and bringing her food they became convinced she was a witch. Children would sneak up on her and throw stones and call her names and soon the village decided that they would kill the fox as they believed it was a creature of the Devil.

A hunt was organised and soon the fox was running for its life chased by the baying hounds and after many hours the hounds cornered him and were going in for the kill when suddenly Rowena was there in the midst of them. She snatched her dying fox from the jaws of the hounds and held him high above their gaping mouths. The hounds were called off and everyone became very afraid of tall Rowena cradling the dead fox in her arms. They turned and almost ran back to their homes. Rowena took the fox home and buried him in her garden.

But that's not the end of the story," Sophie's Nan said. "In a way it's only the beginning, because even though everyone had seen the fox die, it was soon evident that somehow he was alive and well and breaking into their chicken coops and stealing their chickens. The Lord of the Manor was furious because he was losing his pheasants.

The game-keeper was sent to search Rowena's cottage to see if she had somehow nursed him back to health and was keeping him. Of course they found nothing but were not convinced even when shown the fox's grave. But the killing of the birds went on and so a huge hunt was organised by the villagers, and people from all around were invited to join them.

They rode out from the village green and the hounds soon picked up the scent and were off! They chased the fox for mile after mile over hill and through valley, all day. It was dusk when the hounds cornered the fox in the woods. The horsemen were far behind at this point, their horses tired out and when they caught up with the hounds they expected to find the torn body of the fox, but they found the hounds milling around in a puzzled way, as if trying to pick up the scent again and instead of the body of the fox, there was the dead body of Rowena Reynolds, her clothes torn and ripped but not a mark on her. She was buried in the woods not in hallowed ground around the church."

"That's such a sad tale Nan," Sophie exclaimed. "You've not told us that one before."

"Was it the Foxham woods where she died?" Roxy asked.

"Oh yes dear."

"Then it's a true story?"

"Apparently there were no more chicken raids after Rowena's death, so...who knows."

"Not a very cheerful story for a Winter afternoon Helen," said Sophie's Mum. "I hope you girls don't get nightmares." She rose and began to gather up the cups, saucers and plates taking them to the tiny kitchen area to wash them up.

Helen got up and drew the curtains against the darkness.

"I found an injured fox," Roxy almost whispered. "She died in my arms." Helen turned and looked intently at her.

"And do you dream about her?"

Roxy bit her lip and nodded "Quite a bit...she was so beautiful."

Helen patted her arm and smiled "We must have another chat...very soon."

Sophie's Mum bustled in "Come on then girls put your coats on." And turning to Helen gave her a huge hug. "We'll see you again soon and maybe we can hear one of your more cheerful tales."

Helen smiled "I'll see what I can do."

CHAPTER 21

The next couple of weeks sped by and then, it was December and everyone at school was talking about Christmas. Some students were going away for the holidays skiing, while others were off visiting relatives. The ones who were staying were all looking forward to the Boxing Day Hunt...a huge affair where people gathered at the hall from miles away, the Hunt was followed by a ball at Overton Hall and 'anyone' who was 'anyone' would be there.

Roxy listened in silent horror, but noticed with interest that Sid didn't join in the conversation much, in fact he seemed quite withdrawn.

"Are you going to be at the ball this year Sid?" Melanie asked "Or are you having a party again like last year?"

"I'm not going to the ball," he said shortly. "And I don't know about the party." He got up abruptly from the table and made his way towards the doors.

"What's up with him?" Melanie raised her eyebrows. "We all had such a great time last year. Sid smuggled in some wine and we all got a bit drunk, Charles got really drunk and passed out on the sofa." She giggled. "His parents had to carry him to the car!... What are you staring at 'Foxy'?" She glared at Roxy. "I don't suppose you'll be invited. It costs a fortune and you have to have a long gown, not just a party dress."

"Well that's a relief," Roxy retorted. "I can't think of anything worse than spending a fortune on dressing up and then getting drunk." She rose from the table and went out into the fitful sunshine. Sid was sitting hunched on the low wall and Rob seemed to be talking very seriously to him. She didn't go over, it was nothing to do with her, but she had noticed a change in Sid over the past few weeks. He was much quieter at school and didn't show-off as much, and had stopped teasing her altogether.

Roxy found Sophie and spent the rest of her lunch break chatting with her and her friend Lucy. Neither were going away for Christmas, so they agreed to meet up sometime in the Foxham cafe.

***

When Rob and Roxy were upstairs that night in the turret room doing their homework, Roxy asked Rob what they were talking about at lunchtime. Rob was a bit hesitant at first.

"Sid's been having some odd dreams recently, that's all."

"What sort of dreams?"

Rob shook his head slightly. "I don't know whether I should say, he'd hate it if everyone knew."

"Rob, as if I'm going to blab!"

"Yeah, well. He said it felt as if he was a... fox, outside, wandering about. Nearly every night, but once during the day! I think he's a bit scared."

"Roxy's eyes went wide. "Dreaming do you mean?"

"He seems to think it really happens."

Roxy remembered the tale of Old Mother Reynolds and a cold shiver trickled down her back.

"I'm not surprised he's scared. I'd be terrified if that happened to me! What's he going to do about it?

"That's just it, he doesn't know."

"What about his parents?"

"He definitely doesn't want them to know."

"I'm glad he feels he can trust you Rob. I wonder what it's all about though. You don't think it's me banging on about fox hunting do you? I'd hate to be the cause."

"Well, I don't think it helped, but I'm sure you're not to blame. Something else has triggered it."

***

To Roxy's surprise they were both invited to go riding with Sid the following Saturday as there was no football and Sid was obviously not joining the usual Hunt.

Roxy agreed to go, much to Rob's surprise.

"What's made you change your mind?"

Roxy wrinkled her nose. "I don't know; he hasn't had a go at me for ages and... I think because of what you told me. I may be able to help. He needs friends just now, doesn't he?"

They left early and walked over to Sid's across country, it only took them twenty minutes. Sid seemed really pleased to see both of them. Rob rode Nightmare as usual and Sid gave Roxy a grey mare called Pearl. They set off along a Bridle path that ran beside the fields in the direction of Foxham. Soon, past the village, the ground opened out and rose steadily to scrubby moorland sprinkled with rosy clumps of heather...the Foxham Downs.

The horses broke into a canter. Roxy could feel Pearl's sheer delight at racing free and gave her, her head, galloping along, turf flying up behind with the impact of her hooves. The boys raced after her, the ground rising steeply towards the top. Roxy slowed and let the boys catch up.

At the top was a stone pillar. Roxy slid off Pearl's back and went to examine it. There were carvings on all four sides, soldiers, sailors and airmen on three sides and some writing on the fourth side.

"In memory of those who gave their lives in the war 1939 to 1945," Roxy read.

"My Dad had that put there," Sid said coming up behind her. "In memory of my Grandfather. He was a pilot and fought in the Battle of Britain."

The horses were quietly cropping the grass as the youngsters caught their breath and looked with interest at the memorial pillar.

"I can't imagine what it must have been like," Said Roxy. "They were all so brave."

"I expect they were excited too," Rob joined in. "It must have been amazing, flying in those little planes.

You'd get a real sense of flying, not like in the big jets that take you on holiday."

"But they were not all like that," Sid interjected. "Some were terrified but still had to go and fight. They were the bravest of all, I think." Roxy looked at him curiously wondering if he was talking about someone he knew.

"Shall we get on now?" Rob didn't like standing about.

"OK, we'll ride along this ridge, past the old quarry and when we get near the bottom there's a hedge and wall. We can practise jumping. That OK with you, Roxy?" She nodded, dragging her eyes away from the spectacular view spread out below them of stripy fields, the criss-crossing black bare-leafed hedges, the distant hill crowned with Winter trees and above them the immense expanse of blue sky, stretching forever.

They cantered down the hill, Sid leading the way. At the bottom was a hawthorn hedge, red berries like beads decorating the winter twigs. Sid sailed over followed by Rob and Roxy, then across the field and over a wall. Sid slowed to a sedate walk through the next field and led them to the gate into a quiet lane and turned back towards Foxham.

"Is it OK to ride across farmland like this?" Rob asked.

"They're our tenants," Sid said. "It's alright at the momen, they haven't put the ewes in here yet. We won't be able to when they do. Shall we stop off at Foxham and have a coke or something?"

They trotted into the village. It felt strange to Roxy being here on horseback with the villagers staring at them. They tethered the horses and followed Sid inside. He was greeted with a certain amount of respect by the cafe owner and that felt odd too. They bought their drinks and sat at a table in the window. The boys began to talk about the upcoming match next Weekend. As Sid was captain, he had quite a bit of say in who played and in what position. They discussed various players as they sipped their drinks.

Roxy found her thoughts drifting away to the story of Rowena and thought it would be great if Helen wrote them down. She had a wonderful way of telling the story. Then her thoughts jumped to Sid and his dreams. Was there a connection?

The shop bell tinkled and three girls entered. Roxy recognised one of them as Melanie the girl who teased her at school, the girl who 'fancied' Sid.

Melanie's eyes narrowed as she recognised Roxy, then opened wide in a beaming smile at Sid.

"I thought I recognised the horses out the front," She exclaimed, walking towards them. "These are my friends Jane and Louise. They're visiting for the first time. I offered to show them around."

She pulled out a chair from the nearby table and sat down beside them, the other two girls followed suit.

"They go to Mossby Lady's College and are only here for the weekend. This is Sid," she said turning to her friends and indicating Sid with a wave of her hand. "His father is Lord Overton-Croft who owns most of the land around here and lives in that big house I showed you, and this is Rob and Foxy, oh I'm so sorry, Roxy." She gave a simpering giggle and rolled her eyes. "I always make that mistake." Roxy just gave her a blank stare.

"Is it because of the colour of your hair?" Louise asked. "It's a very bright red, I mean is that why you make the mistake?" Louise looked from Roxy to Melanie and back again.

"No," said Sid. "It's because Melanie's being rude!"

Rob burst out laughing seeing Melanie's surprised expression.

"That's not very nice Sid, you know it's because of her 'thing' about foxes," Melanie smirked, her cheeks going pink.

"I can speak for myself you know!" Roxy cut in.

"Well, what is it about foxes?" Jane asked, brushing back her long blond hair and looking at Roxy with steady grey eyes.

"I just think they shouldn't be hunted by dogs." Roxy really didn't want this conversation again.

"I agree," Jane said. "It's totally unacceptable." Roxy stared in amazement.

"Jane!" exclaimed Melanie. "How can you say that. You live in the country, it's part of country life, tradition and all that. Rob and Roxy come from the town it's natural they wouldn't understand."

"Excuse me! What's there to understand?" Roxy's voice had a hard edge to it. Sid put a restraining hand on her arm. He could see her temper rising. Melanie noticed his gesture and she pursed her mouth, her eyes spitefully narrow once more. But it was Jane who spoke.

"It doesn't matter where you come from to recognise cruelty when you see it."

"Can we talk about something else now?" Louise piped up. "This is getting all a bit heated. Anyone fancy a cream cake? I'll pay." She got up from the table and Melanie, casting a caustic glance at Roxy, followed her to the counter muttering angrily in Louise's ear. Sid squeezed Roxy's arm.

"Time to go I think?" There was a twinkle in his eye. Rob pulled a face.

"Nice to meet you Jane," said Sid. She smiled and looked back at Roxy.

"I'm with you on this Roxy. I know it's still going on in spite of the ban." She called.

Outside, Roxy heaved a sigh of relief.

"Sorry about that," she said. "I didn't want to make a scene."

"You didn't do anything," Sid assured her.

They remounted and returned to the stables at the Manor. They unsaddled the horses and gave them a rub down making sure they had enough hay and straw.

"What are your plans for Christmas?" Sid asked as he rubbed down Hero.

"We don't do a lot. Mum likes to put up decorations and have a tree. We'll be able to have a bigger one this year as the lounge is much bigger than the one in town," Said Rob throwing a rug over Nightmare's back. "What do you do? I expect you have a big party and things like that as your Dad's Lord of the Manor."

"We do have a big party on Boxing Day where all the councillors and 'big wigs' come...more like a ball really. I don't go to it. Last year I had a party."

"And got everyone drunk. I heard," Roxy cut in. "Melanie thought it was good fun."

"Yeah, well I thought so at the time, wanted to liven things up a bit. But Dad was furious with me afterwards. Anyway it's usually my job to go out and pick a Christmas tree. Do you want to come? You could choose one too."

"Where do you go?" asked Rob.

"The other side of the wood, there's a fir plantation."

"I know it," Roxy piped up. "Been through it."

"When did you go down to the other side of the wood?" Rob looked at her quizzically.

"One Sunday morning," Roxy could feel her colour rising knowing that Sid would realise she'd been there when he was out walking. She bent down to grab a blanket to throw over Pearl's back hiding her face. Sid gave her a penetrating stare.

"Anyway," he said, seeing her heightened colour and keeping to the subject. "Do you want to come and choose a tree?"

"Yeah, great, when?"

"Let's go tomorrow afternoon. Do you want to come Roxy?"

"Why not."

CHAPTER 22

In spite of all the fresh air and galloping across the countryside, Roxy had difficulty falling asleep that night. She'd seen a different side of Sid today and wondered what it was that had changed him. Was it those very real dreams he was getting? And then her mind turned to the legend of Rowena Reynolds and wondered was it at work once more? This time, somehow working through Sid. She decided she had to talk to Sophie's Nan and find out if there was a way of stopping the dreams, but without telling her why she wanted to know.

Roxanne wondered if, instead of dreaming, Sid was actually out there, in the woods, in the form of the fox. This was all so strange. She went to the window and looked out, thinking she might see a fox loping down the drive as before, but again there was nothing.

Rob too was having a restless night. He was having difficulty believing any of it and thought perhaps his friend was ill. Maybe Sid should give up hunting for a while and just concentrate on football. That would take his mind off things. With this comforting thought, he turned over and went off to sleep only to dream of Sid, in fox form, being chased around the school field by all his class mates and Rob was running after them trying to stop them by yelling "It's Sid! It's Sid!"

Sid meanwhile was tossing and turning in his bed, unable to sleep at all, indeed, he felt more awake than he had done in the day. The urge to leave the house was so strong. He fought it at first, but in the end gave in, dressed, grabbed his trainers and tip-toed downstairs. Using one of the side doors, crept out.

There was no moon, the night deeply dark, apart from the myriads of stars, like a gauzy veil, flung across the blackness of the sky. Frost glittered on every frond of grass and shimmered along the twigs and bare branches. He made his way to the tall chestnut trees that lined the driveway, desperate to change. If anyone had looked out a few moments later they would have seen, lit by the glimmering starlight, a fine dog fox trotting down the driveway then gathering speed before racing off in the direction of the distant farm.

***

Not surprisingly Rob slept in late and breakfast was well under way by the time he arrived downstairs in the kitchen. He slumped into a chair.

"Too much fresh air?" his Mum asked.

"I didn't sleep very well. Did you sleep alright Roxy?" he asked looking at his sister who was munching toast and flipping through the Sunday magazine.

"OK," she answered not looking up.

"I had a few scary dreams," he grumbled, tucking into the egg on toast his mother placed before him.

"Dreaming?" his Mum said. "That's not like you."

"No, anyway Sid's taking us Christmas tree hunting this afternoon," Rob announced to the room in general.

"Oh, where's that then?" His Dad asked joining them at the table and picking up the newspaper.

"The other side of the wood, apparently there's a bit of a fir plantation and we can choose what tree we like and bring it home."

"Are you digging it up or just chopping it down?" His Dad wanted to know.

"Don't know, depends on its size I suppose."

"Could we have a bigger tree this year?" asked Roxy joining the conversation and putting the magazine aside. "We've got a lot more room."

"We don't want a huge one," their Mum exclaimed. "Think of all the dropped needles I'll have to clean up."

"Get the children to clear them," said their Dad disappearing behind his newspaper. Then glancing up, "Homework first."

***

Sid was prompt at two o'clock. He arrived carrying an axe over his shoulder.

"Are you safe with that?" Rob asked him.

Sid pulled a face at him. "I've used it before."

The twins grabbed their coats, scarves and gloves, Rob carrying a spade, and rushed out into the cold, crossed the road and were soon in amongst the trees. Rob noticed the fresh mud on Sid's usually immaculate trainers, but said nothing. Rob and Sid were soon discussing the match that they'd watched on television. They supported different teams but both were doing quite well. Roxy pushed ahead knowing exactly where to go, following the path she'd used before. Sid called out to her.

"Not that way you're leaving the main track."

"This is the way I went before," she said, forging ahead.

"It's a fox's trail," Sid exclaimed wrinkling his nose.. "Can you smell it?"

"Pooh! It's strong!" exclaimed Rob. They arrived at the fir plantation very quickly.

"That was good going Roxy," Sid remarked. "I'd not noticed that track before."

"The fox comes down here in the hope of catching a squirrel. The squirrels come for the fir cones. Look you can see where they've nibbled them." She bent down and picked up a fir cone that had been nibbled down to the main core and handed it to Sid.

"You know a lot about wild animals don't you? for a Townie." Sid grinned at her, teasing, and turning the remains of the cone in his fingers.

"Which trees are we looking at?" Rob asked. "The light will be going and it'll get dark."

"Yeah, the smaller trees are this way." Sid led them to the outskirts of the spinney where there was a swathe of trees varying in height from about two foot to eight foot. The trees were lovely, very symmetrical in shape, with plenty of space between each one.

"Not too big Mum said," Roxy reminded Rob who was gazing in awe at a beautiful fir at least six feet high.

"How about this one?" Sid pointed to a smaller one with elegantly spreading branches. "We could have a go at digging that one up, then you can plant it in the garden," he suggested. So the two boys set about digging up the tree, taking it in turns. In the end Sid had to chop some of the roots or else they would have been digging all night.

Roxy wandered in and out of the trees kicking aside the piles of dried needles and cones that lay about the floor of the wood and examining the fallen logs for fungi. Sid chose his tree and swung the axe several times before it toppled.

"How are we going to get it home?" Rob asked.

"We don't. We'll leave it here for now and I'll send someone down to pick it up tomorrow." They began to make their way back through the wood, the two boys carrying the smaller tree between them. Roxy marching ahead.

"I've never seen you in muddy trainers," Rob remarked, looking pointedly at Sid's feet. Sid stopped and looked at Rob.

"So?"

"Just wondered, that's all if you've been...you know, wandering about in the night."

"It's not something I want to talk about right now," He flicked his head in Roxy's direction. Rob shrugged.

"OK but she's really good at understanding things. Maybe she could help. I'm no good."

Roxy wandered on oblivious, every now and then stopping to look at the black polka dots of old rooks' nests that spotted the twiggy tree tops, or examine where a deer had been nibbling the bark of a tree. Soon the boys were striding ahead once they were on the main path and Roxy was left dawdling behind.

They heard the sound of a woodpecker drumming and the haunting cry of a barn owl taking its first flight in the late afternoon dusk.

"Come on Roxy, it's getting dark!" Rob called. Soon she emerged from the wood, crossing the road and caught them up in the driveway. They carried the tree into the lounge in triumph. But were greeted with loud cries of dismay from their Mum.

"Look what you're doing! Bringing in all that mud and soil over the new carpet!"

"Take it round the back boys till we find something to put it in." Dad ordered.

"We thought you'd be pleased! It's a great tree. The best we've ever had!" Rob exclaimed, disappointed at their response.

"Yep, it's a lovely tree, but round the back please." With Rob groaning in protest, the boys carried it out of the front door once more then round to the back of the house.

Roxy made the three of them hot chocolate and they sat at the kitchen table, Sid having regained his usual confidence regaled them with stories of his exploits at his last boarding school, till the twins' Dad came in, and after thanking Sid for the tree, offered him a lift home.

Rob glanced at Roxy when they had left.

"Did you notice how muddy Sid's trainers were?" He gave her a meaningful stare.

Roxy frowned and shook her head. Rob went on.

"I think Sid was out again last night, you know being a fox," he whispered. "His trainers are always immaculate."

"Did you ask him about it?"

"Yeah, he said he didn't want to talk about it in front of you. I told him you're good at understanding that sort of thing and that you might be able to help."

"What did he say to that?"

"Nothing, we called you to catch us up." He sighed. "I'm out of my depth with this stuff, but I'd like to help him."

"He's got to want help first Rob. The thing is," she hesitated. "I discovered a legend in the museum that might cast some light on the problem, but it sounds so far-fetched."

"It can't be more far-fetched than what Sid believes is happening to him." Roxy took a deep breath and related the whole tale to Rob. His mouth fell open in amazement.

"And you think it's happening again...to Sid? She nodded.

"D'you know how to stop it?"

"No that's the point. I wasn't looking for that at the time. I'll have to have another think."

CHAPTER 23

Sid gradually realised that he could no longer fight against the urge to change into a fox. In fact, he now looked forward to his night time prowls which were fast becoming more real to him than his life as a boy. He loved the challenge of hunting birds and rabbits, he loved his supple body and the enormous strength of his legs. He could leap a six-foot fence easily and run for miles without getting tired. The farmer and his gun were scary but he had managed to raid his hen coop the other night and suffered no damage to himself. He knew he was strong, bold and intelligent. He loved to stand at the top of Brock Hill and bark shrilly into the night telling the world that he was there and afraid of nothing.

The result of his night-time rambles made him irritable and bad-tempered at school. He lacked concentration, and was frequently in trouble with the teachers... his homework was not being done. When his Father received a letter from the school, Sid was in serious trouble.

"What's going on Sidney? You wanted to go to the local school and not boarding school, and promised you'd work hard, and now I get a letter saying your homework's not being done and you're not paying attention in class. Do you want me to find another boarding school for you, where they are even more strict?"

"No Dad, please don't do that, I'm sorry. I'm not sure what's up. I'm not sleeping very well," he shrugged and frowned. "So I'm tired all the time."

"Mmm you are looking a bit washed out. Maybe a chat with the Doctor?"

"No, I'm fine I'll make a real effort to catch up with my work. Maybe Rob could help me. He always gets his homework in on time and I think I would be able to concentrate better if there was someone working alongside me."

"Huh! I'm not convinced. I'll give Justin a ring though, and see what he says."

After his chat with Justin, Sid was allowed to go home with the twins to do his homework, on the understanding that if things didn't improve, a new boarding school would be found and he would go after Christmas.

***

So life took on a new pattern. Sid joined the twins after school. He loved the cosy meals around the kitchen table and the chat and banter, the parents sharing stories about their day. Sally telling them about the various schools she had been working in and Justin about life in the Retirement Home; the jobs he had to do and things he managed to fix to make the elderly people's lives easier. Sid realised that he had been quite lonely in his big mansion, his parents busy and distant, not sharing their lives with him like the twins' parents.

As soon as the meal was over they were sent off to do their homework. Sid loved the turret room. An extra table had been put in for him but it didn't feel crowded. Several of Roxy's paintings and sketches were often lying about or pinned to the wall. Sid could see she was quite talented. He particularly liked the firework painting. It was very unusual with each face reflecting the colour of different fireworks which were shooting up in the background.

"I like that," Sid said, then coloured slightly remembering their argument.

"Oh, thanks," she replied, not looking at him.

It was good to be able to discuss what they had to do. Sid soon discovered that Rob was quite haphazard in his approach, not giving anything much thought, just getting it done, whereas Roxy was very thoughtful and spent quite a bit of time thinking and making notes, sometimes using her Mum's computer to look things up and do a bit of research.

Sid often stayed on when the work was done and they had hot chocolate and biscuits for supper, Roxy curled in the armchair sketching or writing and the boys sprawled on the sagging sofa playing one of Rob's electronic games.

One particular night Sid seemed more withdrawn that usual.

"What's up?" Rob asked, watching him stirring his chocolate around and around staring down at the bubbles. "Is it those dreams again?"

Sid's sharp indrawn breath gave Rob the answer. "Don't worry about Roxy she won't blab."

Roxy looked up from her sketch pad, "What kind of dreams?"

Then Sid told them everything; how it had started with vivid dreams, but then, by finding his feet covered in mud as well as his hands and fingers, his pyjamas smelling strongly of fox and worst of all a taste of blood in his mouth, he began to suspect there was more to it. The twins were horrified.

"How often has this been happening?" Rob asked.

"Quite often. As I said, it started with dreams, but when I found my feet all muddy and my hands, I knew it was becoming real. I usually dress now, when I feel it coming on, that's when you noticed my muddy trainers Rob. And then I became aware of wanting to change, so I do, and now I can't stop it happening. I am aware that I'm doing it. I sprint down to the Chestnut trees, transform, and off I go, then change back in the shadows of the trees in the avenue then sprint up to my room via the side door. I have to go to the bathroom to wash before I get into bed, and rinse that awful taste out of my mouth, or Mum would find out. The thing is, I don't want to stop now, I look forward to changing. It's really exciting."

"That's crazy Sid! You can't live your life like that!"

"And what about the Hunt?" Roxy cut in. "There's a big one on Boxing Day isn't there?"

The boys looked at her, horror dawning in their faces.

"Yes, but I'm supposed to be riding that day. I haven't changed during the day for a while now."

"But you just said you can't help it," Roxy pointed out.

"I do have a certain amount of control, but I have to fight against changing because... I want to transform so badly."

"Well, you'd better be sure not to change on that day." Rob said. "I'll try to keep an eye on you."

Sid gave a crooked smile. "You're a great mate Rob."

The twins' Dad called up the stairs. "Time to go Sid. Done all your homework?"

"Yes Mr Hetherington, on my way."

He gathered up his books, stuffed them in his bag and went down the stairs.

Rob and Roxy stared at each other in silence after he'd gone.

"Well, what do you think?" Rob asked Roxy. "Do you think he's mad?"

"No, I don't. I believe him. He's not the sort to make things up that are...fanciful like that. He's very down to earth. Well, has been till now."

"What do you think then?"

"This is going to sound crazy, but I think something happened to him the day he and his uncle killed that fox I found. The fox was looking right at him when she took her last breath, sort of breathed over him. He's been odd ever since. And I can't stop thinking about the legend."

"So what can we do about it?"

"I don't know yet. I think I might have to go and see Mrs Lawson again, Sophie's Nan, and see if she knows how we can get Sid back to normal."

"You're going to tell her!" Rob looked horrified.

"Don't be daft! I'll ask her in a round about way. I won't say his name; I don't have to be specific."

"Bed-time you two!" Their mother called up the stairs.

"OK we're going!" they shouted back.

Chapter 24

The other youngsters in the class had noticed a change in Sid's behaviour. He was no longer the class joker, and spent more time with Rob and his close football friends kicking a ball around on the school field, when they weren't having training sessions with Mr Turner. Rob, with Sid's permission, spread the word about that Sid's Dad was threatening to send him away again if he didn't settle down and work. So his classmates asked no more questions.

Thursday, after school, they had a match on the floodlit pitch. Rob was now a forward, Sid the striker. The team played well passing to Rob whenever they could, who, if he couldn't score himself managed to get the ball to Sid who was deadly accurate and between them they won the match easily. The whole school seemed to have stayed behind to watch, and was jubilant at their success.

Sid's Dad had even turned up. Sid nudged Rob when they were coming off the pitch amidst cheers and shouts.

"Dad's checking up on me with Mr Turner," Sid said nodding in their direction.

"Well he'll have nothing bad to say, will he, You're 'Man of the match'... and turning your work in on time."

***

On Friday Roxy was lucky. She was chatting to Sophie at lunchtime when Sophie happened to mention that they were having to go to her other grandparents at the weekend because her Grandfather was not well.

"So we won't be able to visit Nan this weekend," lamented Sophie. "She so looks forward to our visits."

Roxy had been racking her brains as to how she could visit Mrs Lawson on her own, and here was the perfect opportunity.

"Would she like me to visit her? I know she'll miss

seeing you and your Mum, but I could do my best to cheer her up."

Sophie jumped at the idea. "Would you Roxy? That's so kind. I'm sure she'd love to see you again. She always asks after you when we go to see her." So it was settled, Roxy was pretty sure her Dad wouldn't mind taking her to visit Mrs Lawson.

***

The rain was rolling down the window panes in wriggling rivulets on Saturday. Large pools had gathered in the dips in the driveway and along the gutters beneath the grass banks, reflecting the dismal charcoal sky smudged with chalky clouds, and the bare branches and twigs of the nearby trees. If you gazed into them long enough the ragged flight of rooks skimmed across the surface.

Roxanne loved gazing at the upside-down world imaged in the pools, she felt she was peeping into another universe. Thinking these strange thoughts as she gazed from her bedroom window she realised that somehow they had already entered a different universe, with Sid and his extraordinary problem.

After lunch Justin drove her to the Retirement Home to see Mrs Lawson. The Old lady was delighted to see her.

"They rang yesterday and told me you were coming. I was so pleased. Oh look how wet you are! Take off your coat dear and hang it in the bathroom. It can drip quite happily in there and hopefully be dry before you go home."

That done they settled before the cosy fire. Helen had made a pot of tea and produced some iced cakes set out on a pretty china plate. She prattled on about the weather and her little plot of garden and asked Roxanne all about school before bringing up the subject that Roxanne most wanted to chat about.

"Last time you came you were particularly interested

in the legend of Rowena Reynalds. Was there any special reason for your interest?"

Roxanne told her about her revulsion of fox hunting and her desire to see it banned completely and how there were loop-holes in the law so it was still going on.

"That's not the only reason though is it dear?" she asked quietly. Roxanne hesitated for a moment.

"No it isn't."

"Are you having vivid dreams?"

"I have been dreaming a bit...yes. But it's not me, it's a friend. It's like the story has come to life again and he actually becomes a fox, mostly at night but also during the day and we're afraid he'll be a fox on Boxing Day."

Helen frowned with concern. "You'd better tell me the whole tale. What kind of boy is he and what does he think of fox hunting?"

So Roxy related what he was like when she first met him and how he had changed recently, and all the events from start to finish.

"So he was there when the fox died? Close to it?"

"Yes, the fox seemed to stare at him just as she died. Sort of trying to communicate with him in an odd sort of way." Roxy coloured feeling that she was being a bit fanciful.

"I'm sure she was. Now, how to stop this thing happening." Helen pondered. Roxy was so pleased that Helen took the whole thing seriously and didn't think Roxy was weird or making it up for a joke.

"Do you think it's some sort of magic curse?" Roxanne whispered.

"Certainly a curse of some sort. Now my dear I think you have some 'digging' to do, and I don't mean in the garden." She smiled at Roxy. "No doubt you know how to use the reference section of the library?"

"Yes"

"Well, I think you will find a book there written by

Thaddeus Crawford. He was a professor of ancient myths and stories in the eighteen hundreds. He was very interested in magic and spells and things and made a collection of them recording them in a book called... 'Spells and Curses Good and Bad' I think. The answer to your problem might be in that book. You could try it."

"I will, that's really great. Thank you so much."

There was a tap at the door. It was Roxanne's Dad.

"Hello Mrs Lawson, have you both had a nice time?"

"Very nice, thank you, Mr Hetherington," Helen said. "Roxy's been telling me all about school and how much she loves the countryside. So good of her to visit, makes the weekend a bit shorter. It would have seemed very long without any visitors at all."

Roxy fetched her coat from the bathroom, it was almost dry, and thanking Helen and giving her a hug, she left with her Dad promising to visit again.

CHAPTER 25

Time was running out. School was breaking up on the twenty first, so there was only a week left before Boxing Day.

"I'm going into town on Wednesday," Roxy told Rob. "Mrs Lawson's suggested a book from the library that might sort out Sid's problem. Do you want to come? We've got Christmas shopping to do as well."

"Yeah, I'll come, But I don't want to spend all my time in the library."

Roxy huffed at him. "You don't need to. I'll do the research you can do your shopping. I'll join you later. We can have lunch in MacDonald's, or KFC."

The last day of term they had a film in the morning and a form party in the afternoon. Everyone contributed food. The form room had been decorated a few days earlier with streamers and fairy lights brought in by some of the girls. They pushed the tables back and played music and danced about in the middle of the floor to silly party songs, everyone doing the movements to go with the song and shouting out the words in a loud off-key chorus.

Sid appeared to be back to normal, showing off again and flirting ridiculously, with every girl. Rob sat watching him, shaking his head.

"He's back to being the class celebrity isn't he!" Rob chuckled to Tom, one of his team mates.

"I don't know; he's been a bit odd recently. It's good to see him back to normal. Let's go and join the circle."

They got up and joined the throng in the centre of the room, bouncing up and down and shouting in raucous voices. Melanie had twisted her arms around Sid's neck. Roxy and Sophie were bouncing up and down across from Sid and Melanie.

"Oh, looks like Melanie's dreams have all come true tonight," Sophie nudged Roxy and nodded in Sid's direction.

"Mmm they make a lovely couple," Roxy replied laughing. "She's only about the sixth girl that's twined herself around him."

The music finished and Mr Turner brought the celebrations to an end. Everyone was expected to help clear up which they did. The boys pushing the tables back into their correct places, the girls dealing with the leftover food and placing all the paper plates and rubbish in black plastic sacks. When everything was back to normal they all left wishing each other and Mr Turner a 'Happy Christmas'.

Sid walked out with Rob, Roxy and Sophie.

"You did alright with the girls again Sid," Rob remarked elbowing him in his side.

"I didn't get to dance with everyone. Roxy didn't dance with me." Sid replied sending her a sideways glance.

"No," she said giving a dramatic sigh. "Shame, I didn't get the chance to tread on your toes."

"I'll look forward to that at my Boxing Day party," he replied looking at her steadily. "Do you want a lift by the way? Mum's picking me up today."

"Thanks," the twins replied.

"I've got to wait for my Mum," Sophie said. "Text me when you want to meet up Roxy," she called.

"Will do! Merry Christmas!"

They bundled into Sid's Mum's car.

"So you're having a party on Boxing Day then?" Rob asked Sid. "Thought you weren't going to bother this year."

"He wasn't going to bother," Sid's mother interrupted. "Because of last year's fiasco. This year, he's promised there'll be no wine."

Sid was pulling silly faces in the back seat. The twins tried hard to keep straight faces.

"I can see you Sid." Two eyes in the rear-view mirror glared at him.

"Sorry Mum," he mumbled lowering his eyes.

"What are you two up to tomorrow?" he asked.

"Christmas shopping," groaned Rob.

"Great, what time?"

"We want to get there by ten thirty," Roxy broke in. "If Rob can drag himself out of bed. We're having lunch there. I want to go to the library as well."

The car pulled up in front of their house and the twins got out.

"Meet you in MacDonald's at one," Sid said as they turned to go into the house.

***

The next day Rob and Roxy caught the bus to Crowhampton, rather later than Roxy hoped as Rob had trouble getting out of bed, it being the first day of the Christmas holiday. They arrived at eleven thirty and Roxanne made straight for the library while Rob walked towards the Shopping Centre.

Roxy asked at the main desk in the reference section for the book Mrs Lawson had recommended. The librarian frowned.

"I've not heard of that one before, but I'll have a look for you." After a while she straightened up from her search and went to a back room. Roxy waited patiently until the lady emerged carrying a large leather-bound tome in her hands. "You know you can't remove it from the library dear, as it's a reference book and a bit of a special book. You'll have to look at it at one of the readers' tables."

"That's fine," Roxy replied taking the book from her and moving to one of the tables.

The book wasn't easy to read as the language was old fashioned but Roxy found what she was looking for in the index, a chapter on breaking spells and curses. She turned quickly to this section, scanning the headings... 'How to Break the Curse of Boils', 'How to Break the Spell of a Love Potion', and so on, and so on.

Then a section on animals and their maladies, breaking the curse on chickens who won't lay, and cows that won't give milk and finally a bit about transforming into animals; a long paragraph on werewolves which involved a ritual performed before the rising of the moon. It sounded very nasty.

Roxanne read further till she came to the section dealing with transforming into a fox. This was not very specific. No ritual was involved and it talked vaguely about the need for the person to experience great fear in order to expel the spirit of the fox. That was all it said.

Roxanne sat back, disappointed, then, caught sight of something written in faded brown ink in the margin. She stared hard turning it this way and that and eventually deciphered the loopy writing. It said, 'Fear of the hounds drives out the spirit of the fox.' A tremor of alarm shivered down her spine. Did it mean what she thought it meant?

"Well that's a bit scary," She muttered to herself. She returned the book and wandered out winding her scarf closely around her neck.

CHAPTER 26

A Christmas market was in full swing outside the Town Hall. Holly and mistletoe in wreaths decorating the stalls. She wandered between the booths, then decided to see if Harry and Marie were there. They remembered her and offered her a coffee. They had been very busy, as the fox hunting season was in full swing, visiting various hunt venues. So far they had been unable to find evidence of any fox being chased and killed, although violence had broken out between the saboteurs and the hunt on three separate occasions.

"So your parents weren't keen on you getting involved then?" Harry smiled kindly. Roxanne shook her head.

"I did go to the Hunt at Foxham, but Dad insisted I stayed near him. We only watched them set off. They followed a trail. My brother took part. I was pretty mad at him."

"Hi Roxy!" The voice made her jump, she spun round. Sid was standing behind her. His eyes caught the posters, and as he looked, his face drained of colour.

"Sid! You're early!" Roxy could feel herself blushing. "Marie, Harry this is Sid. We're meeting Rob to go Christmas Shopping. I'll say goodbye for now." She turned back to Sid who was still fixated on the posters, and touched his arm. "Shall we go?" He blinked and his eyes focused on her face.

"Yeah...sorry." He looked really shaken.

"What's up?" Roxy whispered.

He gave a huge sigh. "Those pictures...brought back an awful memory, that's all."

"Do you want to talk about it?"

"Yeah, let's go for a walk, it's ages till lunch."

They walked down the hill until they came to a park that used to be the grounds of the ancient abbey. They sat on one of the benches and Roxy waited patiently for Sid to explain, glad to see he'd regained some of his colour.

"I thought you were going to pass out, you looked so white."

"Yeah it was those pictures, it reminded me of my first hunt with Dad. We did chase a fox and the hounds got to it before we did. It was torn to bits." He covered his face with his hands, as if to blot out the sight. "But the worst thing was, Dad, cut off the tail, and because it was my first hunt tried to smear my face with the blood. They call it 'Blooding'. I was hysterical and Dad was very angry with me. I've never forgotten it, but lately it's come back really vividly along with all these other odd things that are happening. I think I'm going mad and... it's scary."

Roxy was shocked at the brutality of Sid's father. "I wouldn't be surprised if all these happenings are connected in some way with that experience," she said.

"But it happened such a long time ago."

"But sometimes these things surface later in life, maybe when your body thinks it's able to deal with them." She looked at him cautiously. "There could be another explanation." She hesitated.

"Go on," Sid gave her a sharp stare.

"I think something happened that day the fox was killed. It seemed to breathe on you as it died and these strange things have been happening to you since then. It might seem a bit far-fetched but when I was looking into legends and things surrounding the area I came upon an old story about a woman who seemed to have the ability to change into a fox and raid the neighbours' chickens." Roxy had Sid's full attention now."

"Go on," he said again. "What happened?"

"Well, it happened after a hunt, the hounds caught and killed her fox, but the chicken raids went on. So they organised another hunt and again the hounds caught the fox but when the riders got there it wasn't the body of the fox they found, it was the old woman."

"So they believed that this woman changed into the

fox." Sid finished the story.

Roxanne nodded, her face solemn.

"OK, so have I got to be torn to pieces to stop this happening?" He looked angry now, his eyes flashing.

"No, but the answer's not very helpful."

"Great!"

Roxanne went on in spite of his interruption. "There was this writing in the margin of another old book about curses. It said, 'The terror of hounds drives out the spirit of the fox.'"

"Terror! That sounds fun." He blew out a huge breath in a despairing sigh. "So how's that going to happen?"

"I was thinking that maybe... it's got to be the Boxing Day Hunt."

"You're kidding aren't you? You want me to be the fox at the Boxing Day Hunt, and get chased and possibly killed? I thought you two were going to stick by me and make sure I didn't change on that day."

"We can still stick by you," Roxy cut in hurriedly. "We can make sure we follow the hounds really closely so we keep up with them, and be there to rescue you from them."

"We? You and Rob together? Hunting a fox?" His old mocking tone was back. "What would Harry and Marie think?"

"Do you want help or not?" Roxanne's colour was rising as was her temper.

He sighed and lowered his eyes.

"Of course I do, but I'd prefer an easier way. I don't fancy being scared out of my skin."

"We'll talk to Rob over lunch and make a plan." They left the gardens and headed for the town centre.

Rob had grabbed a table right at the back. There were mums with small children on the surrounding tables, so plenty of noise to cover what they were going to be talking about. Rob looked at their long faces.

"What's up?" he asked moving along so Sid could sit with him on his side of the table.

"We'll tell you in a minute. What does everyone want to eat?"

Rob went with Sid while Roxanne saved the table for them. After the first mouthful Rob wanted to know what they'd been talking about. So Sid, lowering his voice told him shortly what Roxanne had come up with.

Rob gulped and nearly choked. "That's crazy Roxanne. Can't you come up with anything better than that?"

"Such as? What's your idea?"

"OK let's not get into an argument," Sid commanded. "Roxy's been looking at old legends and stuff and apparently this has happened before and the only way to break the power is by driving it out with great fear. I'm not keen, but I'm willing to try anything."

"What we need is a plan," Roxy said. "We need to find out where the trail goes, and where the fox needs to cut across the trail. So we can make sure that we're close behind the hounds when it happens."

"How about we ride ahead and wait somewhere near the spot where we know the fox will cut across the trail. I don't think we'll be missed. We can be there at the start and then slope off once everything gets under way."

"I can find out where the trail will be laid," Sid offered.

"We'll have to have a look at the map as soon as we know, to plan your route when the hounds have got your scent. The safest idea would be to make for water. They'll lose your scent then once you're in the water."

"Yeah, but this is a fox you're talking about," Rob cut in, he looked at Sid. "Do foxes think like that?"

"It's funny, but when I'm a fox there's still a bit of me that can think like Sid. I know when I've got to change back and go home, for instance. So I could probably decide to make for water."

"Where's the nearest water after the duck pond?" Roxy asked.

"The River," Sid replied shortly.

"But that's miles away!" she exclaimed.

"I'll have to give them a run for their money," Sid answered with a wry grin.

The boys went home once their Christmas shopping was done, leaving Roxy to finish hers on her own. She turned over in her mind all that they had talked about, knowing it was a desperate plan, but the only one they had to cling on to.

CHAPTER 27

Sid fell into a troubled sleep that night and immediately he was deep in the woods, hungry no longer. A plump pheasant had walked across his path. He had pounced, it had tried to fly but to no avail. His sharp teeth had sunk into its neck and it hung limp and warm from his jaws. The tearing of the flesh and crunch of fragile bones had been a joy to him as his empty stomach filled. He huffed away some of the feathers but swallowed others along with the fine satisfying flesh of the bird.

Sid's eyes flew open with horror. The slight memory of an aftertaste made him want to vomit. He hurried to the bathroom and swished ice-cold water around his mouth before spitting it out. He sat on the edge of the bath trying to banish the images that kept flashing into his mind. His dreams were so real, the smells, the tastes, the feel of the undergrowth, the cold dampness beneath his paws. So sleep brought him no peace, there was no escape from this nightmare. He became a fox in his dreams. He had paws and a long bushy tail and a thick coat of fur, just like the times when he wasn't dreaming, when he really did become a fox. The memory of the legend flitted into his mind, the old woman had died!

He went back to bed only to succumb once more to the dreadful urge to make his dreams a reality and fully change into the form of a fox.

***

He padded softly down the drive towards the road, taking a track that led up to the Downs. The turf was short and rabbit nibbled, gorse bushes cast dense shadows across the gravelly stones as the waxing moon shone with a bright haloed light. He reached the monument and sniffed around it, vague memories stirred, of a boy and girl and horses. He paused at the quarry, deep in shadow, a black abyss. He threw back his head and barked a shrieking bark an anguished lament. Something distressing had happened here, he felt a strong and tragic loss but had no real memory of it. He trotted on down the hill, past a blasted oak tree where an owl hooted from the dead branches, and entered a spinney of trees. He avoided the large badger that was foraging among the leaves and headed for the village where he could be sure of a tasty meal.

On reaching the village he jogged up the empty High street, leapt over a wall into a back garden. The dustbins were full and overflowing. He eased off the wobbly lid and pulled out half a cooked chicken and a bag of stale doughnuts. He ate what he could tearing at the paper bag with his front paws leaving the bits scattered over the yard.

The sky was beginning to glow in the east so he turned for home knowing he had to reach the avenue and change before the sun came up. It was going to be a glorious winter day. He loped along, racing the sun.

***

That afternoon Roxy was going to the Christmas party at the Cedars with Sophie and her family. They picked her up after lunch. The party started at three o'clock.

The main sitting room was decorated with streamers and garlands of holly. A huge tree, reaching almost to the ceiling, glittered in one corner bedecked with tinsel and fairy lights. Along one wall, tables were laid with plates and trays of sandwiches, cold meats, quiches, sausage rolls, cakes and gateaux of every description, not forgetting mince pies, and in the centre, a massive Christmas cake covered in white icing and decorated with silvery snowflakes. A lady was playing a medley of carols on a piano that stood in a corner, adding to the festive atmosphere.

The room was packed with family and friends of the residents, everyone dressed in their best. Roxy was welcomed warmly by Mrs Lawson, just like one of her family. They sat around her on comfy chairs chatting quietly, waiting for the proceedings to begin.

The manageress came in and everyone stopped chattering to listen to what she was about to say.

"Welcome everyone," she began "So nice to see such a large crowd joining us for our Christmas celebrations. We are beginning the afternoon by joining our pianist, Mrs Windthrop, in a selection of Christmas Carols. Shall we give her a welcome?"

Everyone clapped loudly. They spent the next twenty minutes singing all their favourite Carols: Silent Night, Hark the Herald, Little town of Bethlehem, Once in Royal David's City. Carol sheets had been handed out but most of the residents seemed to know them by heart to Roxy's amazement.

The Carol singing was followed by a surprise visit from Father Christmas who handed out small gifts of sweets, and chocolate to everyone. After that, crackers were pulled and paper hats crowned each elderly head, plates handed out and the wonderful feast was begun, after which dance music was played and several couples got up and waltzed around the room. The men looking very upright and sprightly, the ladies very feminine in their smart dresses.

Mrs Lawson managed to ask Roxy whether she'd been successful in finding the book and hopefully the answer to her friend's problem. Roxy was just about to tell her, when Sophie's Dad leant forward.

"Mum, would you like to dance?" Helen beamed at him.

"I would love to, Son." He took her hand and led her onto the floor. Mrs Lawson looked back at Roxy who smiled and nodded.

The party ended and all the visitors began to drift out to their cars, saying fond 'goodbyes' and calling 'Happy

Christmas' to everyone. Helen was going home with Sophie and her family to spend Christmas and the New Year with them.

CHAPTER 28

The next day was Christmas Eve and Sid sent Rob a text asking if they would like to go riding again. The sun was shining. There had been a sharp frost in the early morning, freezing any pools or puddles. A thin skin of ice covered the pond and the ducks quacked miserably on the bank, or waddled perilously across its slippery surface.

The twins' Mother was quite happy to drop them off at the big house.

"I've loads to do for tomorrow, and I'll get on quicker without you two hanging around," she laughed.

Sid was already at the stables when they arrived. He looked dreadful, white faced with dark rings beneath his eyes. He tried to give his usual carefree smile, but failed utterly.

"You look rough mate!" Rob remarked. "You look as if you haven't slept."

Sid shook his head. "I haven't. I'll tell you later let's go."

He'd already saddled up the three horses, Pearl for Roxy, Nightmare for Rob and Sid's favourite, Hero. They mounted and trotted out of the stable yard and down the drive turning towards Foxham Downs. They rode in silence aware that Sid wanted to talk but was struggling with how to say it, so was concentrating on his riding. Once on the Downs they broke into a hard gallop, racing each other to the top by the memorial pillar. Sid reached it first and dismounted, sinking down onto the grass with his back against the pillar. Rob and Roxy joined him.

"Come on then, spit it out, what's up?" Rob demanded.

"I had the worst night ever last night." He puffed out a long sigh. "As soon as I got into bed and fell asleep I was dreaming I was a fox again. I dreamt I'd been eating a pheasant, it was disgusting." He grimaced at the thought. "I could taste its blood again!" He shuddered. "I had to rinse my mouth out to get rid of the taste. Then, when I went back to bed, I knew I was going to transform. I couldn't stop myself. I was out all night. I was eating out of the village dustbins! It makes me feel sick just thinking about it!" The twins listened in silence.

"Well," Rob stammered. "It's not for long. It'll all be over, the day after tomorrow."

"That's just it… I don't think I can go through with it. We don't even know whether it will work and there's the Meet, Dad and Mum will be looking out for me. They'll expect me to be there...and wonder where I am if I don't turn up." He stared hopelessly at the ground in front of him.

"You have to go through with it," Roxanne cut in. Sid's head snapped up, looking her in the face. "It's all we've got to go on. Otherwise you'll continue to transform into a fox and who knows, maybe one day you won't transform back." Her tone was hard.

Sid's eyes narrowed as he looked at her. "And what if being chased by hounds doesn't work?" he said sarcastically. Undeterred, she shrugged.

"We'll have to try something else. We can't give up at our first attempt."

"But what if the dogs get me first!"

"They won't. Rob and I will get there first. Look Sid," her voice softened. "It's your only chance right now. You've got to trust us."

He sighed again, then pulled out from his jacket pocket a map and the trail plan. "I managed to get these." He threw them on the grass in front of them. Rob opened up the plan as Roxy spread out the map and they compared them. It was a long trail, passing two other villages and circling the farm and school, then doubling back, skirting the wood and returning to Foxham. They studied the map intently.

"I know how we can fool your parents into thinking you're at the hunt." Roxy said. "Rob can borrow you jacket and ride Hero. If he keeps his distance no-one will know, they'll just see the horse and assume it's you. I'll ride Nightmare and everyone will think I'm Rob. They won't expect me to be there."

"That's a great idea Roxy," Rob said enthusiastically. "That'll work." Sid looked slightly more cheerful, esteem in his eyes.

"You'll have to lie low until you hear the hounds, but as soon as you do, you can lead them a 'merry dance', like foxes do, but make your way to the river. We'll meet you by this bridge here." She pointed to a small bridge, quite a way upstream from the bridge at Crowhampton. "We'll have to hobble Pearl in Badgers' Spinney when we change horses, then when we come to find you, we'll bring her with us and re-join the hunt or go back to your place."

"What's this about Badgers' Spinney?" Sid was looking really confused.

"You'll have to go early to Badgers' Spinney on Hero, and tether him for Rob to ride, leaving your jacket for him to wear. Then transform and leave a bit of a trail for the hounds to pick up, then hole up somewhere till you hear the hounds." Roxy spoke slowly, watching to see if Sid was fully comprehending what she was saying. "When we arrive to pick up Nightmare and Pearl we'll tell the grooms that we're catching you up or something like that, then we'll ride to Badgers' Spinney, hobble Pearl, so she won't wander, Rob will change into your jacket and mount Hero, I'll mount Nightmare and we trot back to join the Meet outside the pub keeping our distance from everyone who might look too closely."

"Wow Roxy, that's a great plan. You've thought of everything!" Rob was full of admiration.

"How long has it taken you to work all that out?" Sid asked equally amazed.

"I haven't been sleeping much," she grinned.

"I'm grateful, considering what a rat I was at first."

She nodded. "Mmm...you were rather." They smiled

at each other.

"What'll you do about your hair?" he asked flicking the ends with his fingers. Roxy's hair was long and curly.

"I'm going to plait it and wind the plaits around my head and jam my riding hat on over the top. It should work."

"Can we just run through everything again?" Rob asked. "I want to make sure I know exactly what's happening.

"OK, I'll start," said Sid. "I leave home early on Hero, ride to Badgers' Spinney, tether Hero, leave my jacket, transform, lay low after leaving a bit of a fox trail, run like hell when I hear the hounds, make for the river, cross it and meet you on the other side by the bridge. Your turn."

"OK, we arrive at the stables," Rob continued. "Tell the groom we've promised to meet up with you… ride to Badgers Spinney… change jackets and ride Hero, um… Roxy rides Nightmare and we join the Meet, keeping out of everyone's way."

"You forgot Pear,." Roxy said.

"Oh yeah… hobble Pearl."

"We follow the hunt until the hounds take off after the scent of fox. When that happens, we make straight for the bridge to wait for Sid. We might get there before you." she said looking at Sid.

"Hopefully," he replied, fear shadowing his eyes once more. "We'd better get back," he said rising to his feet. "Look at those clouds."

A huge bank of threatening purple clouds was massing on the horizon beyond Crowhampton and was moving towards them as the wind grew in strength. The sun went out like a blown candle and branches were soon whipping about seeming to scribble across the sky. The horses stamped and whinnied not at all happy with the change in the weather.

"It looks like we're in for a snow storm." said Sid

throwing himself into the saddle. But it wasn't a snow storm, it was torrential rain, which thundered down upon the land, turning fields to muddy lakes and swelling the river that swirled in angry torrents, rising inch by inch up the banks, the currents strong and furious.

CHAPTER 29

They arrived back at the stables drenched to the skin. Sid and the twins helped the grooms take the horses into the stables to dry them off with rough towels before blanketing them and leading them into their stalls. Then they trooped into Sid's huge kitchen and had a hot drink before the twins rang their Dad to ask for a lift home. They gave each other meaningful looks as they said their goodbyes.

"See you at the Hunt," Rob said slapping Sid on the shoulder.

"Yeah, right, see you, have a good Christmas Day."

"You too!"

***

The twins rushed upstairs to change as soon as they got home. The rain was still coming down in sheets and every now and again there were brief flashes of lightning and the distant roll of thunder. It rained steadily for the rest of the day and all through the night. There was fear of flooding.

It had stopped by the time Christmas morning dawned and a pale sunshine sparkled on each twig and branch and the pools were bright, reflecting the pearly grey sky.

"Breakfast first," said Justin, sitting down at the kitchen table where Sally, still in her dressing gown, joined him.

"What's it to be?" asked Rob, assuming the role of a waiter.

"Oh, I think we'll have the 'works'," Sally replied. "Bacon, eggs, sausage, mushrooms, tomatoes, fried bread, what else have you got?"

"Fried potatoes," Roxy called from beside the cooker.

It was a family tradition that the children prepared

breakfast for their parents on Christmas Day. Delicious smells rose into the air as the bacon and sausages began to cook.

When breakfast was finished they trooped into the lounge and sat around the Christmas tree. Rob was the 'postman' this year and duly handed out the presents one by one. They never gave extravagant gifts, especially this year, having recently moved house, so they were mostly useful or fun. Justin had a brand new tool box, his old one was beginning to fall apart. The twins had bought him some new screwdrivers and secateurs. He was delighted.

For their Mum, a new cookery book entitled "Country Cookery" with fabulous illustrations and recipes from famous celebrity chefs. Roxy received a wonderful book called 'Country Matters' all about conservation with a list of conservation groups in the back. She was absolutely thrilled. Rob had a book tracing his favourite football team's history and some new football boots.

Apart from these main gifts there were scarves and gloves and chocolates and silly slippers in the shape of animals and a new board game called Ingenious which was a bit like dominoes but much more complicated with different coloured tiles.

Roxy helped her Mum prepare the vegetables while their Dad took care of the turkey and Rob washed up the utensils, bowls and dishes as they were used. Then, he opened up the game and worked out how it should be played, reading all the rules and how to score, ready for the evening.

The table was laid in the dining room which they hardly ever used. The polished table covered with a festive cloth and the best china, glasses and cutlery were brought out as it was a very special day - their first Christmas Day in their new home. The vegetables were brought in, in bowls and dishes and placed at intervals down the table then, Justin came in bearing the turkey. Everyone cheered as he set it down and began to carve. They helped themselves to their favourite vegetables. No-one had room for pudding so it was decided that they would have it at tea time.

As the rain had stopped, the family decided to go for a short walk while it was still light. They donned their Wellingtons or boots and crossed the road into the trees. The paths were very muddy and slippery with rivulets of water running down the centre in some places, but they managed to get to the top of Brock Hill without accident. Neither Justin nor Sally had ventured into the woods before and were thrilled with the uninterrupted view from the top over patchwork fields, now studded with pools after the rain.

The clouds had been ripped apart and driven east. Great shafts of sunlight arrowed down illuminating parts of the landscape, while others remained in dusky shadow. The pools twinkled and glittered in the fields, reflecting the sky and the scudding clouds. A brisk breeze tugged at their scarves and woolly hats, sending roses into their cheeks, numbing their fingers in spite of gloves and freezing their noses. Overhead a Red Kite soared on stretched pinions and the only sound was the wind in their ears and the sweet song of a Robin in a nearby bush.

"This is wonderful!" sighed Sally. "I'm so glad we moved. Why ever haven't I walked out here till now? I never thought Winter could be so beautiful." Justin put his arm around her shoulders and gave her a hug.

"I'm glad you're happy! Oh look!" He exclaimed, "A fox!" Sure enough a fine red fox was jogging across the field skirting the pond and entering the fringe of trees below them. Rob threw Roxy a quick glance, his eyebrows raised in consternation. She frowned and bit her lip.

"Well, I think it's time to return home, before our fingers fall off," Said Justin.

"My nose has disappeared completely!" Sally laughed.

That evening they mastered the new game, with lots

of laughter and cries of frustration and triumph, depending on who won and who lost.

When bedtime came Roxy could feel a tight knot of fear and apprehension gripping her inside. She was dreading the following day.

CHAPTER 30

Sid hardly slept at all. He'd really enjoyed his ramble as a fox that afternoon, the freedom, the feeling of power, knowing his strength and swiftness, knowing that other creatures lived in fear of him, but the knowledge of what was to happen the following day filled him with total terror now. He twisted and turned in his bed fighting the impulse to leave his room, transform and run away completely, never to return. He paced his room wishing Rob and Roxy were with him. They gave him confidence and Roxy always talked sense. He knew what she would say about his crazy idea to change into a fox and stay that way forever. Somehow he had to get through this night without giving in. He picked up his phone and decided to ring her. She answered straight away.

"Sorry, did I wake you?" Sid asked.

"No. I can't sleep either. Was it you we saw today by the duck pond?"

"Yeah, I just had to get out of the house for a bit. Where were you?"

"On the top of Brock Hill. Dad saw you first. We guessed it was you. We went out for a walk. Mum and Dad haven't really been out to explore much. They've both been too busy working."

"I'm a bit nervous about tomorrow."

"So am I, but I'm sure everything is going to be fine," Roxy said confidently. "Our plans are good... they'll work."

"Actually, I'm terrified," Sid admitted. "I'm shaking. I'm afraid to sleep in case I transform... and... the thing is I want to... I want to change and not change back, just run away and be a fox forever."

"No Sid, you can't do that. Think about what it would do to your Mum and Dad and all your friends if you just disappeared without any explanation."

"I don't think Dad would mind much. He always

thought I was the 'runt'. He preferred my brother."

"I didn't know you had a brother. What happened?"

"My father blames me."

"What happened?" Roxy asked again.

"He died… rescuing me from the quarry. I was angry and showing off, as usual. We'd had an argument at home. Dad went on about how amazing Paul was in every way. He was clever and fearless, an excellent rider in the hunt. I became really angry and decided to prove to everyone how brave I was. So I rushed off to the quarry. I had a terrible fear of heights, but I was determined to prove that I could overcome this fear and be as brave as Paul. But Paul must have followed me. He was shouting after me telling me Dad didn't mean what he was saying, but I knew different.

"I went to the edge of the quarry and began to climb down, even though my head was spinning. Then the ground began to crumble away and I slid for several feet before stopping on a ledge. I was screaming. I can still hear myself. I looked up and I could see Paul's face peering down at me. He was as white as a sheet and I realised then, that he was as scared of heights as I was. That's what I meant by real bravery, up by the Memorial stone, still doing the right thing even though you're terrified of doing it.

"I could see he was scared to death but he began to climb down to me testing each step making sure it was safe before putting his whole weight on it, and he made it safely to the ledge. Then he supported me, guiding my hands and feet, as I scrambled back up. I remember reaching the top and just rolling over onto the grass feeling so relieved. I turned towards him as his head emerged above the rim of the quarry. I heard him gasp as he scrabbled for a hand-hold in the grass, but it was too short and slipped from his fingers. I held out my hand to him, but I was too late. The ground had given way and he fell… to the bottom of the quarry."

"Oh God, Sid how awful!" Roxy was appalled. There was a pause as she tried to take it all in. "How old were you?"

"I was eight, my brother was fifteen. He was bright, and hoping to go to university. Mum and Dad were devastated. Father was furious with me, so I know I was to blame, but there was nothing I could do to put it right. I kept saying sorry, but of course it made no difference, and I missed my brother so much.

"They sent me away to school after that. Mum said it was to help me get over it… new surroundings and people. But I carried the ache around inside me for ages… still do in a way. When I'm a fox it goes away completely. I can feel that foxes are used to losing friends and family. It happens all the time to them." His misery and loneliness came over the phone in waves. Roxy took a deep breath before answering him.

"Listen Sid, this is an awful thing that happened. In a way you've not just lost your brother, but you feel you've lost your Dad too, and that's terrible, but I also know that running away from yourself is not the way through to peace, 'cos that's what staying as a fox is all about. Running away from yourself. I know, because it's what I tried to do, to change and be someone different, because I realised I wasn't like most of the other girls at school and they didn't accept me.

"At first I was really unhappy. I didn't fit in anywhere, I was teased and left out. But I realised I cared about different things and enjoyed totally different stuff from them. It wasn't until I accepted this fact, that I found a kind of peace, it was no big deal in the end. I was happy being who I was and I didn't have to change and be like anyone else. I could be me. You don't have to try to prove to your Dad that you're as good as your brother, or go out of your way to be the complete opposite. Just be you… you're great as you are!"

"Mm… That's how you come across, really strong.

You know your own mind. I noticed it the first time we met. Even though you get steamed up about stuff. You don't care if you don't fit in. I'd like to be like that. I could stop playing the fool then." There was a hint of laughter in his voice, he was more relaxed. "I'd better let you get some sleep. Thanks for talking Roxy. I'll be OK now."

"I know you will," she replied, smiling into the phone. She snuggled down under the duvet. How strange she thought, sometimes the people you disliked so much at first, once you know their story, become the ones you like best.

CHAPTER 31

The twins arrived at the stables as planned, having been dropped off by their mother. The day was bright with lawns and grasses paled by frost. Ice rimed the edges of puddles and glazed the distant duck pond. The horses' hooves clanged on the frosty cobbles of the stable yard and everywhere there was noise and bustle as grooms and riders readied their mounts.

No questions were asked as Rob and Roxy appeared and helped saddle Pearl and Nightmare. They rode off with no-one giving them a second glance.

They reached the Spinney. There was no sign of Sid, but Hero was tethered under the trees and Sid's Jacket was draped over the lower bough of one of the trees. Rob changed quickly, passing his jacket to Roxy.

"Is my hair all tucked up under my hat?" Roxy inquired.

"Yeah fine," Rob gave her a hurried glance as he carefully hobbled Pearl, allowing her to move around within the spinney and graze. He leapt onto Hero's back and Roxy mounted Nightmare. They paused looking at each other. Taking a deep breath, they turned, to trot back and join the hunting party.

There was a huge crowd outside the pub at Foxham. The twins made sure that they were far enough away from anyone who would want to talk to them.

A few friends and some people they didn't know waved at them across the melee, they waved back but made no move towards them. Roxy noticed Melanie trying to push her way through the crowd to reach Rob, thinking he was Sid. Roxy leant forward slapping Rob on the back as if he had said something funny and at the same time indicated what Melanie was up to. Rob turned Hero away and pushed further into the crowd. At that point the toast was drunk, the horn sounded and the hunt moved off, clattering down the street in the direction of the Downs.

***

Sid had escaped straight after breakfast and taken Hero, telling the groom he would be back in time for the start of the hunt. If the groom was surprised, he didn't question it.

As soon as Sid reached Badgers' Spinney, he leapt off Hero's back and hobbled him, then slung his jacket over a low branch, he could feel his limbs trembling with the beginning of the transformation. He fell forward again, his arms changing into the fine forelegs of a fox, aware of the trees shooting up all around him again as he shrank, becoming a fox once more. Hero whinnied his disapproval, the fox gave him a backward look and wound his way through the trees towards Foxham Downs, his ears intent and alert to catch the slightest sound of baying hounds.

He trotted leisurely across the fields which were rutted with frozen mud, squeezing himself under the fences, and pushing his way, belly to the earth, through the hedges till the ground began to rise. Here, small pebbles worked themselves loose from the soil beneath his paws and rolled down the slope. The tufts of grass were sparse and spiky with frost.

He stopped at the memorial pillar and sniffed around. Strange memories echoed once more in his head but they made no sense to him now. He passed the lip of the quarry where again a memory stirred and with it a frisson of fear. He quickened his pace, there something he had to do, somewhere he had to be, but the memory had gone.

The frost was melting, and as far as he could see, water glistened in the fields and along the tracks and by-ways. The river, a silver ribbon in the distance, had overflowed its banks and birds were swimming in the new ponds that had been formed in the fields. That jogged his memory. He had to make for the river sometime, but when, he didn't know?

Then, he heard it. Far in the distance the winding of the huntsman's horn and the baying of hounds. He gazed behind him and watched as they flooded across the fields below; the brown and white sea of dogs, noses to the ground, the cantering horses and trotting ponies carrying yelling riders in bright red or black jackets bobbing up and down rhythmically with the movement of their mounts. He waited to see where they were going. They were following another trail, not following him. But as he turned to go down the hill the sound behind him changed, the barking and baying grew much louder and the fox knew they had picked up his scent.

His blood pounded in his ears as his legs stretched forward. He felt a surge of pride at his speed, and joy sang through his whole body as the race was on.

They were a long way behind him as he leapt clear over a fence and dived into some dense gorse bushes. They won't like that he thought. By instinct, he made for an old earth he knew in the bank of some ancient ruins, but when he got there the earth was full of boulders and there was no way in. He ran on and on forgetting, in his panic, where he was supposed to go.

***

The twins had deliberately hung back among the new-comers to the hunt and younger children on demure ponies, and let everyone, including Melanie, who lost sight of them in the crush, streak on before them. The new-comers would not recognise them, but when the hounds had clearly found the fox's scent they cantered towards the front. To their horror they realised Sid had turned the wrong way somehow and was being chased across the Downs, miles away from the river.

"He must have forgotten what we told him. We'll just have to follow to see which way he's going and keep up with the hounds and hope nobody recognises us," Roxanne gasped.

"What an idiot!" exclaimed Rob. "What's he up to?"

They passed quite a few people who, if they had looked closely, would have known it wasn't Sid riding Hero, but luckily everyone was too excited to take much notice. The hounds streamed ahead. When they came to a fence, some jumped over, some scrambled over and some just pushed their way through. Rob and Roxanne soared over with other experienced riders including Sid's Dad.

"That's my boy!" They heard him shout as they cleared the third fence in a row. Rob grinned at Roxy.

***

A gradual thaw had set in and from the heights of the Downs, the ground became increasingly marshy and mud coated his belly. His brush dragged along the ground, heavy and wet, and then it came to him… make for the river! He twisted around and heaving in great gulps of air raced ahead, he could see the river and the bridge in the far distance, where he would be safe, although he had no idea why he thought that. Rob and Roxy had disappeared from his memory.

He raced through the farm yard setting the dogs barking and straining at the leashes and flew into a spinney of trees. The hounds were coming closer and he could feel his strength fading. His pads felt like lead, and his lungs near bursting but on he ran.

Ahead was another village and a road, not busy this day. He streaked across the road and through a church yard, dodging in and out among the grave stones, tried to leap the wall but falling back, then managing at his second attempt, he dashed through someone's garden and pushed under the hedge, causing a hullabaloo as the hounds followed his every move.

He found himself in a straight narrow lane with high

banks on either side, topped with hedges. The lane was less wet beneath his pads and he made good progress, but in the end he needed to climb the bank and enter more open ground. He scrabbled at the slope, slithered and fell again and again. The hounds had entered the lane and were gaining on him. With one last valiant effort he reached the top of the bank and scrambled through the hedge. No time to stop, he bolted across the open field and into the shelter of some trees that led down to the river. At this point a tremendous noise broke out behind him, horns blaring and a lot of banging and shouting, a sense of utter confusion was in the air accompanied by a chorus of angry voices. The hounds baying became subdued, but he didn't stop, he raced on.

For some reason he didn't understand, he knew he had to dive into the river, but to his dismay he realised the river was now a raging torrent, after the rain storm, but he didn't hesitate and threw himself in, trying to swim to the far bank. The current was much too strong and he was swept away downstream, too tired to fight any more.

CHAPTER 32

When the hounds broke free of the narrow lane the hunt saboteurs appeared from across the fields wearing sinister black balaclavas, and striking up a raucous noise, banging tin trays and blowing their own hunting horn. The riders arrived a short time later. There was no sign of the fox. They were furious and shouted loud abuse at the saboteurs and one or two charged at them, but it didn't stop them. The hounds, on the other hand, milled about, confused, not knowing what to do. Distracted by the noise, they lost the scent, amongst the pools that spread across the field like shining mirrors. Then with a great howl, they charged off, turning away from the river and heading back towards Foxham.

All the riders followed whooping in delight, not realising that the fox had gone in a completely different direction, and the hounds were following the original laid down trail. Rob and Roxy were stunned by what went on, but taking advantage of the confusion, raced for the bridge, hoping that that was where Sid had gone, keen to let him know the hunt was heading away from him.

On reaching the bank, they halted in alarm as they edged carefully between the willows, some waist-deep in water, and saw the torrent that was now the river. There was no sign of fox or Sid.

"Would he have jumped in d'you think?" Rob asked in alarm.

"He was a fox… I don't know what a fox would do." Roxy was biting her lips. "If he did, he'd have been taken downstream. He'd never have swum against that current. Let's go to the next bridge and keep a look out. I can't bear this!" she exclaimed "If anything bad has happened it's my fault, I suggested it!"

"You didn't know it was going to rain like that," Rob said as they picked their way through the trees and shrubs, their eyes fixed on the bank, hoping for a glimpse of rusty fur or Sid's white shirt.

Halfway, between the bridges, a tree had come down and jutted out into the water which sprayed up over it like a fountain.

"He's there! Look!" yelled Roxy pointing. Draped across one of the branches, and half in the water, was a figure in a white shirt, not moving. Rob leapt from Hero's back and waded into the water, Roxy followed. It wasn't very deep as they were in the overflow, but they had to tread carefully, unable to see what lay beneath the muddy waters. Rob bent over Sid calling his name.

"Is he OK?" Roxy was near to tears.

"He's breathing… just. He's freezing cold. I can't lift him on my own, I'm afraid I'll drop him in the water when I pull him off this branch."

"I can help." Roxy reached out and grabbed Sid's other arm as Rob eased him from the branch. They dragged him between them up the bank till they reached slightly drier ground. Water poured from his mouth and nose, then he coughed and groaned, gasping and retching. His eyelids fluttered.

"I'm not a fox." His gruff voice croaked.

"No, just very wet mate." Rob was grinning from ear to ear slapping him on the back, causing him to cough and splutter.

Sid turned his head and looked at Roxy, raising his hand, she grasped it in hers.

"It worked… your idea… the fox has gone. I can feel it." He smiled a faint smile.

She gave him a shaky smile back trying hard to stem the tears that were gathering in her eyes.

"You gave us such a fright, when we saw the state of the river. I had no idea…" The tears spilled.

"You wouldn't… you're a townie," he said with his usual grin. Rob helped him to sit up, rubbing his arms to get some life back into them.

"We've got to go and get Pearl. Are you fit enough

to ride?"

"Yeah, I'll ride behind you Rob."

Mounting their horses once again, they set off for the spinney at a gentle trot, Sid gripping Rob's waist and leaning into his back. The hunt had long since disappeared and people were beginning, no doubt, to wonder where the three of them had got to.

They reached the spinney and were able to give Sid his dry jacket to wear. Roxy gave Rob back his jacket and took hers from the branch and put it on, she also shook out her hair from under her hat, no longer having to pretend she was her brother. Sid was shaking by now with cold and shock, his teeth chattering, his skin waxy white. They had to get him home as quickly as possible. Rob and Roxy rode on either side of him to make sure he was safe. They broke into a canter which whipped some colour back into Sid's cheeks, but he still looked blue around his eyes and mouth.

The stable yard was still quite busy as the grooms with solemn faces, moved about tending the remaining horses. They looked around when the three clattered into the yard, smiles breaking out on their faces when they saw Sid.

Sid's father was just about to mount up, preparing to set out to look for him. At the sound of the hooves, his face, grey with worry, changed to one of joy at the sight of Sid, then changed again to deep concern when he saw the water dripping from him and the colour of his face and obvious weakness as he slid from Hero's back. He ran and gathered Sid into his arms.

"I was just going out to look for you. What happened?"

Rob dismounted. "He almost fell in the river... well... he did ... in a way." Sid was shaking so much his knees began to buckle. His father half carried him towards the house.

"Sidney! you could have been drowned. Into the

house with you. You must get warm. Come on you two. What were you doing by the river? You must tell me what happened." He half turned, beckoning Rob and Roxy who shared an alarmed glance, but handed the horses over to the grooms that hurried forwards.

They all went into the kitchen which was warm, and a great fuss was made to prepare hot drinks and bring blankets. Sid was bundled into and ancient saggy armchair when his mother arrived looking distraught.

She gave Sid a huge hug. "Whatever happened to you? We've been frantic with worry. You're soaking wet!" She drew back gazing at him. "You need to get out of those wet clothes." Then seeing the twins, frowned. "You two are wet through too. You need to change."

"He fell in the river. I just wanted to find out how it happened." Lord Overton tried to explain to his wife.

"That can wait Henry, they need to get warm and dry. Off you go now. Ellen will find you some clothes Roxy." With tremendous relief they were ushered from the kitchen, drinks in hand, up to Sidney's room. Roxy was handed some dry clothes which she put on in the bathroom before joining the boys in Sid's room.

Sid had a hot shower which brought him back to life, nevertheless he wrapped himself in his duvet as he cradled his hot drink between his hands. He looked up as Roxy entered after knocking.

"Well, what are we going to say?" He asked. "Dad won't give up till he has a good explanation."

"We lost our way?" Rob suggested hopefully.

Sid pulled a face. "I don't think so."

"You could blame me if you like," Roxy said. They looked at her questioningly.

"How d'you mean?" Sid asked.

"I was thinking that we could say something about me seeing the fox making for the river and going after him to save him from the hounds. You chased after me... Hero stumbled in the water... you fell."

"Mmm, he might buy that," Sid considered carefully. "You don't mind him knowing how you feel about fox hunting?"

She shook her head. "Not if you don't mind him thinking you fell off!"

"OK we'll go with that then." He grinned.

CHAPTER 33

Sid's mother insisted that he rested for the afternoon and when he objected, threatened to cancel the party otherwise.

"Your father rang to find out where you were," she said to the twins "But I told him I'd drop you round."

It was their cue to go. "Sorry," said Rob "We didn't realise it was so late. We should have phoned to let him know we were OK. but our phones got rather wet."

It was half past two when they arrived home and had to explain why they were so late. Apparently the incident at the hunt with the saboteurs had been on the local television news and had been filmed.

"I was terrified that you were involved Roxy. But I couldn't see you. They looked so intimidating in those hoods!" Sally exclaimed. "Then when you didn't come home, I didn't know what to think."

"We rang the Hall and were told Sid was missing too and Lord Overton was going out to look for you all." Justin told the twins.

They kept the details to a minimum, apologising profusely. Both parents were shocked at hearing about Sid's accident but glad that Rob and Roxy were on hand to help him and none the worse for their adventure.

After a late lunch they went upstairs, both tired out and not really looking forward to the party.

"I wonder if Sid's Dad accepted his story," Roxy wondered aloud, plumping down on Rob's bed.

"He would," Rob half chuckled. "Sid's great at spinning a tale." Roxy smiled then stood up and stretched.

"D'you know Rob, I think the saboteurs saved the day. They totally confused the hounds giving Sid extra time to get away to the river. The hounds were so close."

"Yeah, but also the fields were very wet. It must have been difficult for the hounds to follow his scent through the pools."

"They picked up the trail scent though," Roxy argued.

"Yeah they did," Rob conceded.

"Anyway, I think I'll have a rest now, I feel achy all over. What time is the party again?"

"Six o'clock."

***

Overton Hall was lit up like a fairy-tale castle when they arrived, every window ablaze with light. Cars were pulling up disgorging excited teenagers before driving away again, a constant stream of noise and movement. The twins joined the throng moving towards the front doors that were flung wide to welcome them.

The party was held in the large conservatory that ran along the side of the west wing of the house. A band was playing at the far end and coloured lights strobed the dance floor which was already crowded with couples gyrating happily. Sid came across to them as soon as they entered the room and gave Rob a huge grin and flung an arm around his shoulder.

"I haven't said 'thank you'. You actually saved my life." Rob just shook his head and grinned back. Sid looked at Roxy, his face very serious.

"And you, set me free. In more ways than one. I'll tell you later. Now, let's party!" They were soon swallowed up in the crowd, dancing with the best of them, the loud music drowning out any conversation. Rob was having a wonderful time with Jane, Melanie's friend, who was staying for Christmas. Roxy was dancing with Tom when Sid cut in.

He grabbed her hand. "Excuse us mate, need to talk to Roxy." He led her outside and away from the noise and the lights, along the terrace to the far end. A huge moon bathed the lawns and borders in silver light. Clouds sailed slowly in filmy drifts across the sky, a frosty stillness filled the air. They settled on a bench in the shelter of a sweet scented hedge of Daphne and Winter Jasmine.

"What are we doing out here?" Roxy asked hugging herself with her arms.

"I haven't thanked you. Here put this on, you're cold." He took off his sweatshirt draping it around her, his arm keeping it in place across her shoulders. She turned to look at him, her head on one side.

"Was your Dad OK with your story?"

"More than OK. Do you remember what we talked about on the phone the other night?"

She nodded.

"Well as I talked to Dad and he talked to me, I realised, he does care about me, and he understood what happened at the quarry and was actually sorry about being so angry and saying the things he said. To be honest, I couldn't take it all in. We've never had a conversation like that before.

"Also, we talked about fox hunting and I told him exactly what I thought, that I agreed with you, it was barbaric, now I know what it's like first hand. I was a bit scared, wondering how he'd react, but he was OK about it." Roxy stared at Sid in amazement.

"He took me seriously and promised we'd keep strictly to the ban in February. So, that's another great result."

Roxy smiled happily. Sid went on.

"You freed me from changing into a fox all the time. The most exciting, but terrifying thing that has ever happened to me, even my fall in the quarry. The thing is, if that fox hadn't died, none of this would have happened. I wouldn't have got to know you, even though you're a Townie." He grinned teasingly at her. "I'd not have made it up with Dad, I'd still be the stupid… show-off, and no doubt foxes would still be hunted. I'm really sorry about the fox, but tremendously good things have happened because of it. You've helped me see the countryside in a totally different way, a better way. And I'm grateful."

Roxy had no idea what to say to all this, but she had a deep down warm, happy feeling, glad that Sid was her friend. This was the real Sid and she liked him.

They sat in silence taking in the silvered scene spread out before them. The moon lighting up the glassy faces of the frozen pools, the black sentinel trees marching down the avenue, and as they gazed, a wild sound rang out from the hill and echoed across the empty fields – the lonely cry of a fox.

END

Printed in Great Britain
by Amazon

38664834R00085